I0833225

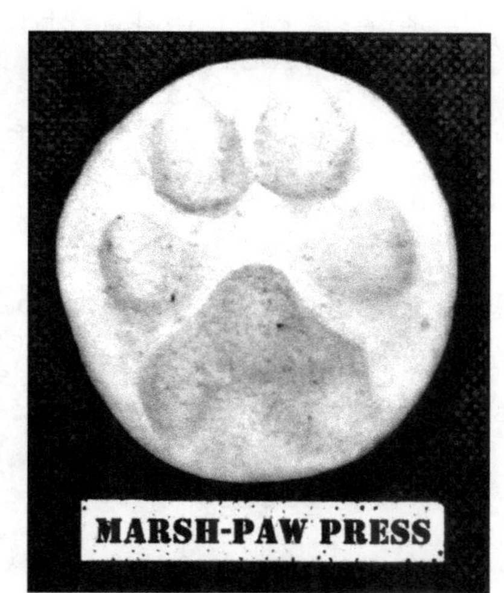
MARSH-PAW PRESS

Other Books by Trevor R. Fairbanks

Novels

Acquaro
Any Mouse
Centipede Sunset
The Defective Man
Dragonmoth and Running Snake
Ex Eyegore
Flyweight
I, Corpse
I Kill for Satan
Joe Smith
Scarwynd
Speed Metal Cowboy
Unraveling the Owl God

Short Stories

Acid Drop
Bloodsucker Blues
Cemetery of the Heart
The Darker Side of God
End of Odds
For Every Awkward Teenager
Gore Suspenstories
Haunting the Library
Infidel
Whorehouse
Johnny Panic and the Necronomicon of Nightmares
Knights in Satan's Service
Love in the Time of Pornography
Son to the Servants of the God of the Dead

Poetry

Epics in Miniature
The First Poet on Mars
The Heretics Bible
The Kamikaze Poet

Other Books by Eric C. Harrison

Blackened White - Art collection # 1

Denizens of Distraction - Art collection # 2

$#&%!!! Art collection # 3

Quirkish Delight - Drawings & Sketches, 2012

Picture of A Paranoid - Poems, Prose & Short Stories, 2002-2012

At The Bottom of The Big Top - A horror story told with poems

Parallel Enigmas – poetry by Carter Monroe & Eric C. Harrison

Finding the Secret Sea

An experiment in spontaneity of image/word association

Art by Eric C. Harrison / words by Mike Maguire

Black Mercury

An Experiment in Spontaneity of Image/Word Association.

Drawings & Sketches by Eric C. Harrison

Words by Trevor R. Fairbanks

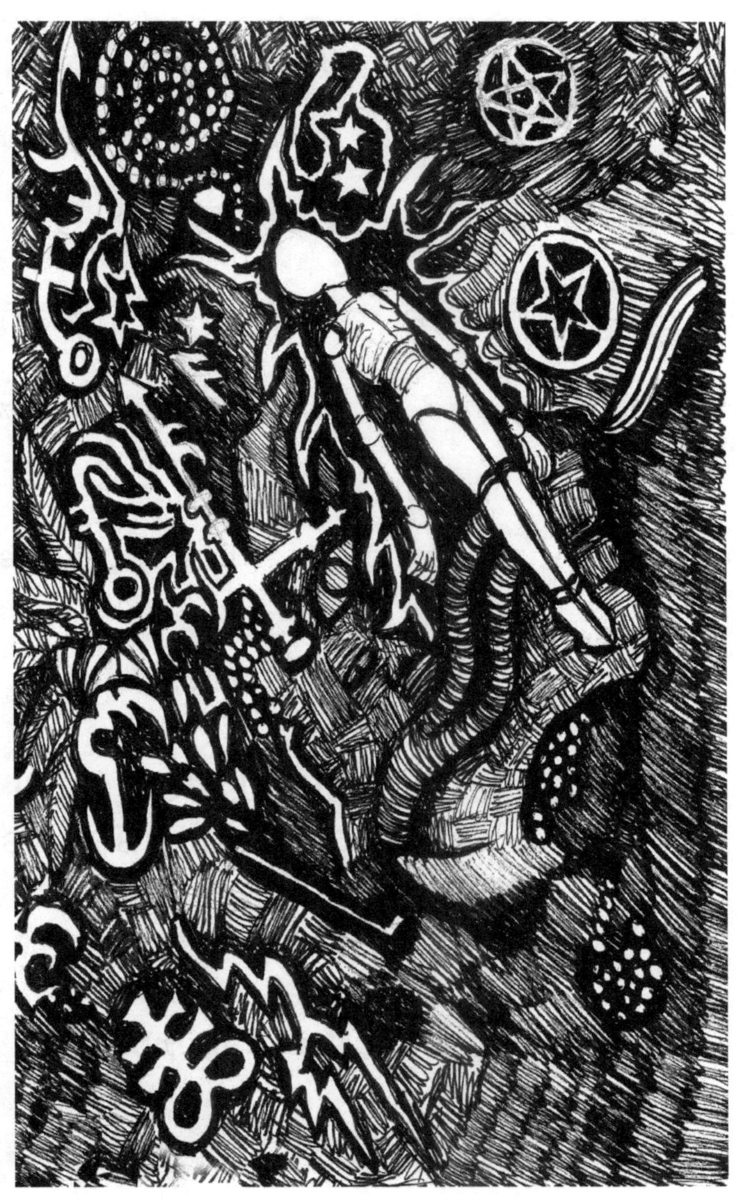

2015

Marsh Paw Press

BLACK MERCURY

An Experiment in Spontaneity of Image/Word Association.

ISBN 978-0-9888040-6-7

Sketches & Cover Art by Eric C. Harrison

Words by Trevor R. Fairbanks

End Notes presented by S. Spectre, Summer 2015

For information, write to - stilldiseased@aol.com

Published by:

Marsh-Paw Press
Saltmarsh, Massachusetts
October - 2015

*** First Edition Paperback**

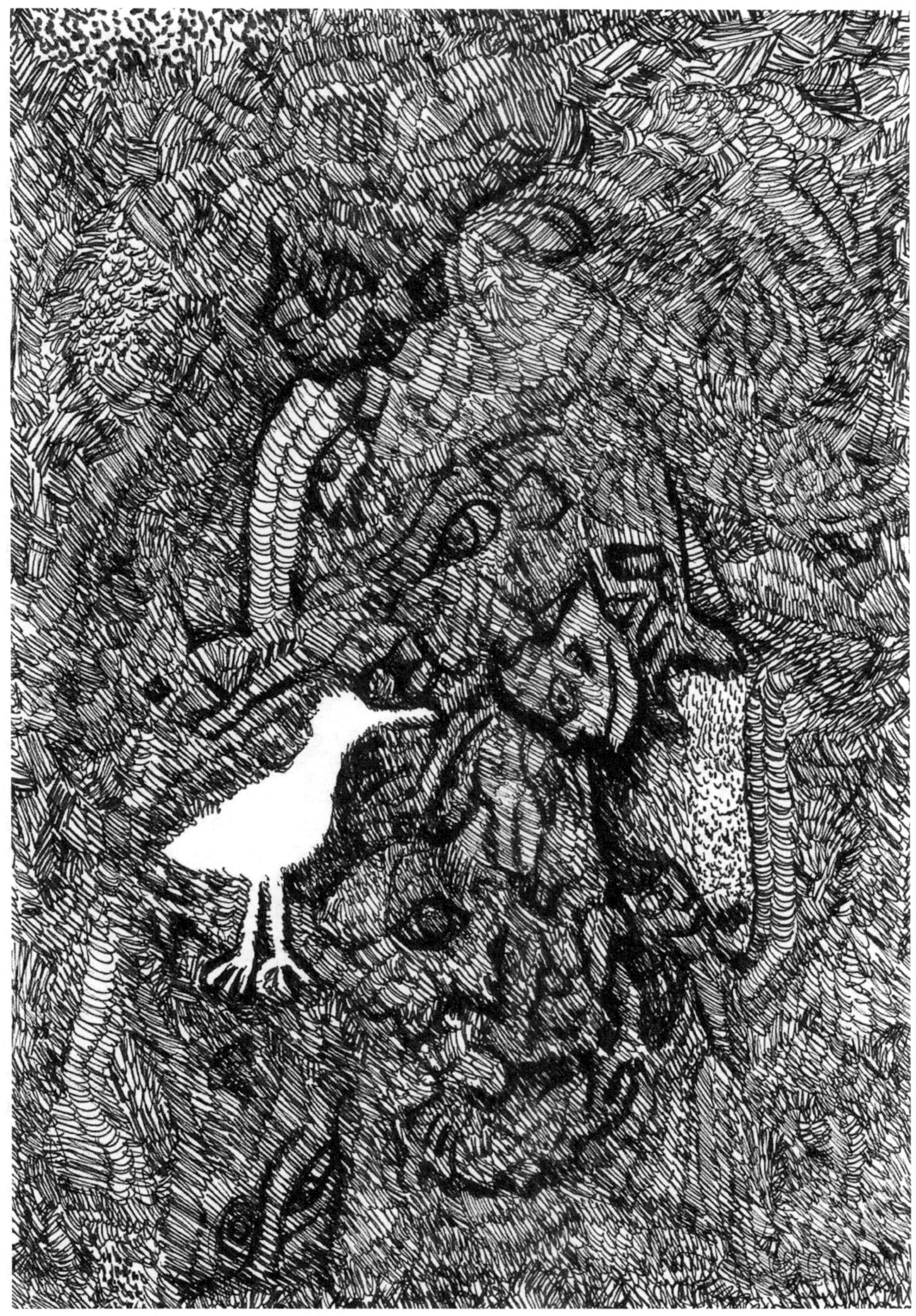

The Fall of the Lightning Lord

No longer would the moist clouds of the eternal realm comfort his sleeping body at night. No longer would the soft rains soothe his aching skin through the harsh summer months. No longer would he wander barefoot across the oceans of unfathomable knowledge, learning about all things that had no meaning. He had come of age. The time had come to mate.

The planet was waiting.

Dark clouds were separated by white hot bolts of electricity as he fell through the atmosphere. The rains that came with the tearing of the sky were angry and violent. These were the type of rains that washed mountains away and drowned entire cities. And the muddy earth that rushed up to catch him was wet and filthy. When he crashed into the ruin the sound could be heard for miles.

The entire world was listening.

For a moment he lay still, taking it all in. The eternal realm was gone now. Soon it would be only a memory. Which was what he wanted more than anything. He wanted to be his own person. He wanted his own life.

He wanted to be the God of a new planet.

But it was pointless to reminisce. He was a boy no longer and he had chosen this world as his own. Now he stood up and wondered what would come to greet him.

The baying of a dog made him turn. He looked into the eyes of the hound and managed to smile. It was a gentle creature, and of natural birth. He could tell by the leaves in its hair that it was one with this world. And it was healthy, which was a good sign. He could tell from the way its tail wagged happily. A good healthy beast meant a healthy world, unless...

"Rx? What did you find?"

There was a light in the darkness. The tiny flickering flame attached to the candle revealed a human.

And he felt his heart sink.

Humans were always a problem.

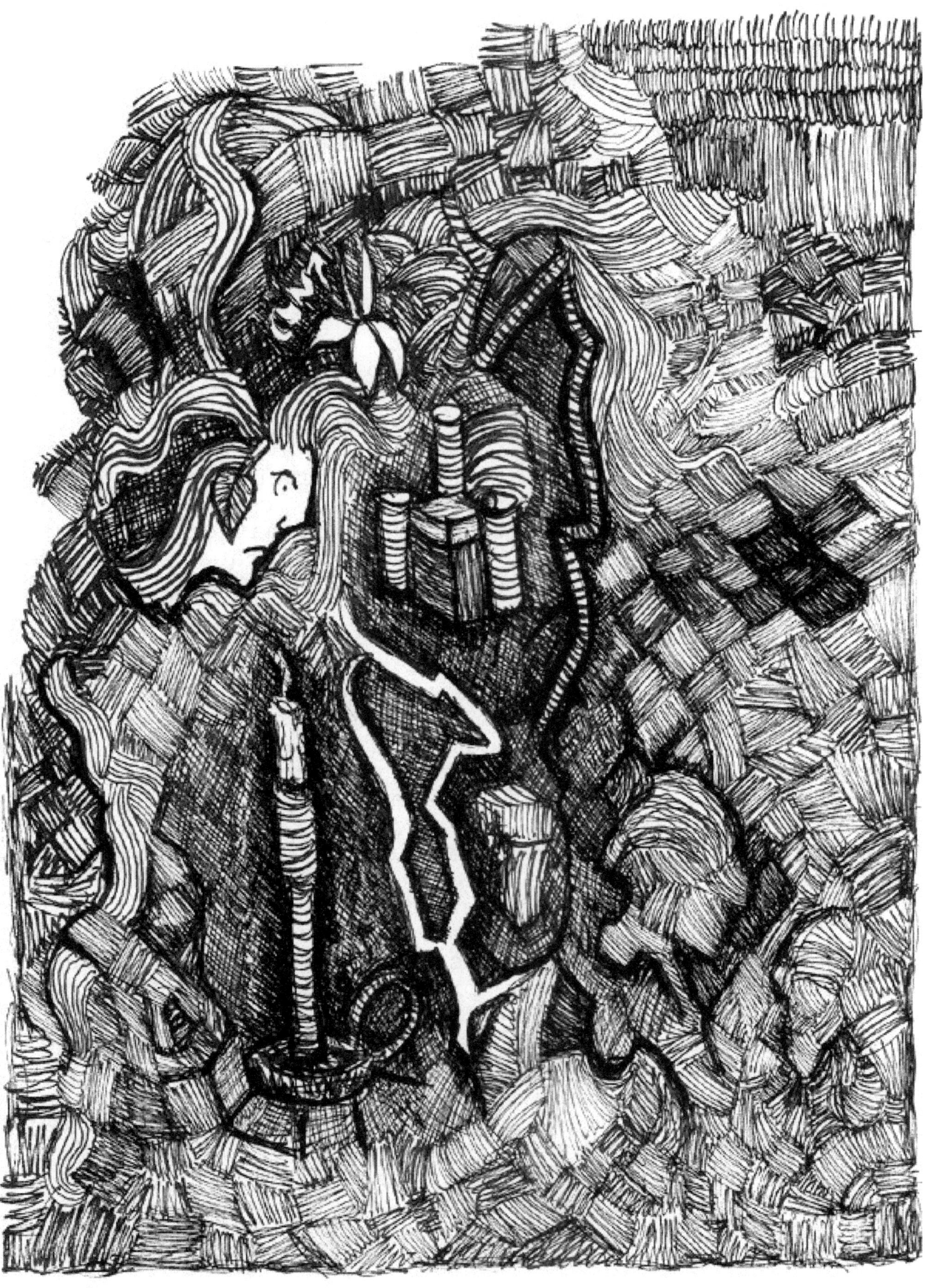

The Infection Speaks

"I have been waiting for you," the man said as he fell to his knees in worship. "Yes. I have been here for so long! How blessed are we! The God has returned to save us all from the torture of life!"

"No, I am ..." But it was too late.

This was the problem with humans. They believed in anything blindly. And even though they were stupid, their beliefs were strong.

His kind fed on those belief. It nourished them. It became them.

Now he was already starting to take on the aspects of what this man believed him to be. A god. The God of...

"My name is Kanker," the old man smiled. "And you are..."

Golden lightning shimmered and started to fade. In its place came white bone and dark clothing. Blood began to flow through new veins. Dark matter coalesced and formed a brain. The flesh on his face was there for a moment before melting away, leaving a skull behind.

His eyes looked out at the planet before turning into dark sockets. Teeth smiled without meaning.

"You are the God of Death," the man said as the dog began to howl. It was no longer friendly and the visitor was no longer welcome. But the man ignored its warnings. "You have come to take me back to her! Please, I must see my wife again!"

There was no use in arguing. It was already happening. And before he knew it the Lord of Lightning was the God of Death.

"Take me!" the man commanded.

"I must rest first," was his reply. Besides, he wanted to see how bad things were on this world. Maybe the infection had yet to spread. Maybe the world could still be saved.

"Oh, of course." The man took a stand and brushed the mud from his pants. "Even a God needs rest, I suppose. Please, come with me."

They started walking and soon the forest gave way to the city.

Things were even worse than he thought. These humans had already started to build colonies. From the looks of things they were not new to this planet. They had been evolving for thousands of years. The infection ran deep.

The city itself was disgusting. Hundreds of doors and stairs crisscrossed a mountainside that was almost hidden under all that concrete. Everything was on top of each other. It was like looking into the face of a disease.

This was the colony.

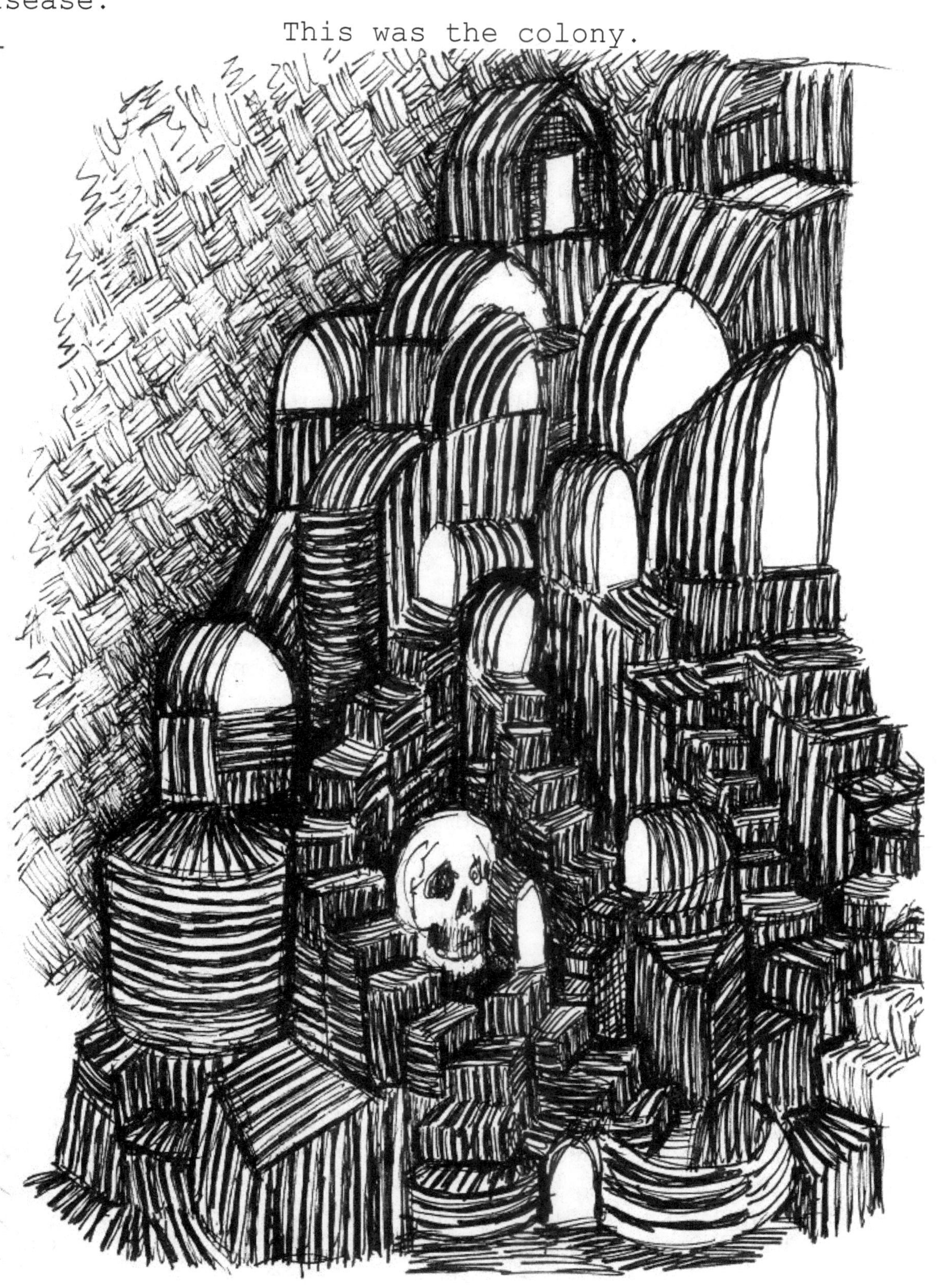

Syphilis

"Syph!" Kanker shouted as they entered his tiny abode. "We have a very special guest. Why don't you bring him something to drink?"

The creature emerged from a hidden doorway. It was emaciated and thin, with great eyes that glowed in the darkness like a firefly's ass. He knew that they could see anything because, like a good slave, they were trained to see everything. And remember. Slaves always had a good memory.

It nodded and drifted away as he and the man sat down at a low table. The dog curled up obediently at Kanker's feet but never let its eyes escape the new comer. Every so often a soft growl rumbled through its chest.

"Syph is just my house-servant," the man said with a proud smile. "Pay him no attention."

But it was not something he could ignore. In fact, he felt disgusted. Obviously these creatures had yet to learn the truth about harmony. They still kept others in slavery for their own needs. It would not have surprised him if they still used money. The thought of it made him sick.

When Syph returned with the drinks he looked at him. "Yes. You are a very interesting guest," the slave slurred his words.

The eyes seemed to glow and he felt himself begin to change again, reconfiguring to suit whatever the slave needed to believe in. The skull was gone, and in its place a man's face with a shackled neck. He could feel whip scars burn across his back. He could feel boils form on his feet and hands from decades spent working in the fields. Suddenly he was no longer a God but a martyr.

"Tomorrow we leave," the man commanded with a smile. He looked at him and wondered where it was that he thought they were going. "Yes. You will take me to the other side, so that I can see my wife again."

"Your wife?"

"She died months ago. I have been waiting for you ever since. Please, you must take me! I must see her! I WANT TO DIE!!!"

Death was still such a mystery for them. They did not even realize that the other side was only another world and it was no better or worse than this one. They were so blind and stupid they could not understand that the mysteries they were trying to solve were not mysteries at all.

"I understand," he nodded and Kanker leaned back in his chair with a satisfied grin. Syph remained in the dark corner, looking at him. His eyes glowed feebly in the darkness. "I will take you where you need to go."

"And me?" Syph asked, his voice croaking from the gloom. "You shall give me what I want, too?"

He looked at this foul creature, this slave. Everything made sense. He could give them both what they wanted.

All he had to do was kill this man, Kanker.

Parasite Symphony

Strange music flowed up through the floorboards like a bad memory. The melodies were haunting in their simplicity, and they reminded him of the sirens off the moons of Luthok. But where their songs were beautiful, this was disgusting. It was a form of music so simplified that it could hardly claim the name. It sounded like animals in a pen braying for release, set to an ass-shaking drum beat that paralyzed the mind into thinking that it had some sort of significance.

"Oh, never mind that," Kanker said, noticing his discomfort. "It's just my downstairs neighbor. He has some peculiar tastes in music."

"He does."

"It's been a plague on my ears for years." The old man's eyes suddenly lit up. He looked upon his visitor and the question fell from his lips like a brick. "Do you think you could ... well, you know?"

"Kill him?"

Kanker grinned and nodded his head with vibrant enthusiasm.

"You are the God of death, aren't you? Go ahead. Kill him."

"No."

Kanker sighed. So did he. These humans knew no better. They thought that they could command the Gods simply by asking.

"My wife loved music. Real music, not that tripe downstairs. I swear she had the voice of an angel. Any chance to sing, any chance! And she would belt out harmonies like you wouldn't believe. But you probably already know that."

He did not, but decided to let the old man have his moment. "Do you truly miss her?"

"Oh, I do! I do! Every day I miss my wife! I would give anything to see her again!"

And who was he to deny him? He looked at the old man. He looked into his old eyes. He decided to give him his dream. "Then join her," he said and snapped his fingers.

A bolt of lightning streaked in through the window. The old man named Kanker was reduced to ash. Finally that annoying voice was silenced. Now if he could just get the downstairs neighbor to stop playing that infernal drum pattern.

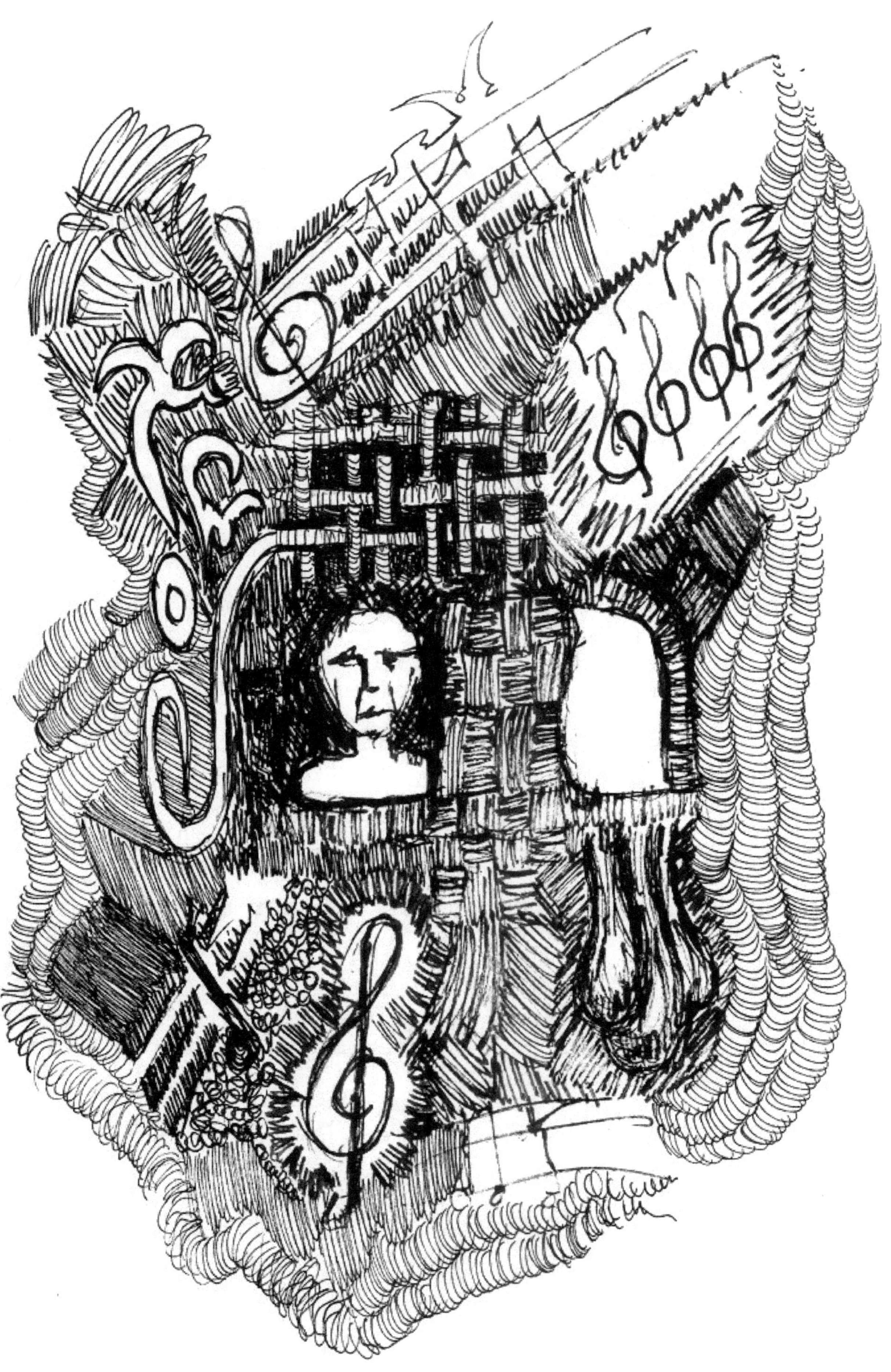

Soulstorm

The smoke was starting to clear. It was arid in his nostrils and delicious. The taste of burnt ozone had always been his favorite and now it was mixed with human flesh. It even had a tinge of charred hair.

He started to relax. Maybe this world was not so bad. Then they started to appear. They came through the charred opening and he realized that the lightning bolt he had thrown at Kanker had obliterated an entire wall of the house.

People were coming through. He looked at them and their dead eyes, staring out from the nothing. They were thin to the point of emaciation, like skeletons. He knew what they were.

Slaves.

"Syph told us about you," one of them wheezed and he felt himself begin to assume the aspect of their beliefs. Only moments ago he was the God of Death, now he was the King of all who suffered slavery. He was a martyr.

And he knew that martyrs did not live forever. In worlds like this they never lasted for long.

"Dreamed of you for a long time," one of them whispered. "Been waiting for you, we have."

"Our sins ... you must die for our sins."

"Then we get to see," another spoke. "The lights. The lights!"

He looked at them. They were holding pieces of wood and long nails. One of them had a crown of thorns clutched reverently in hand.

"The masters," they moaned. "Say you must die. It is the only way to live forever."

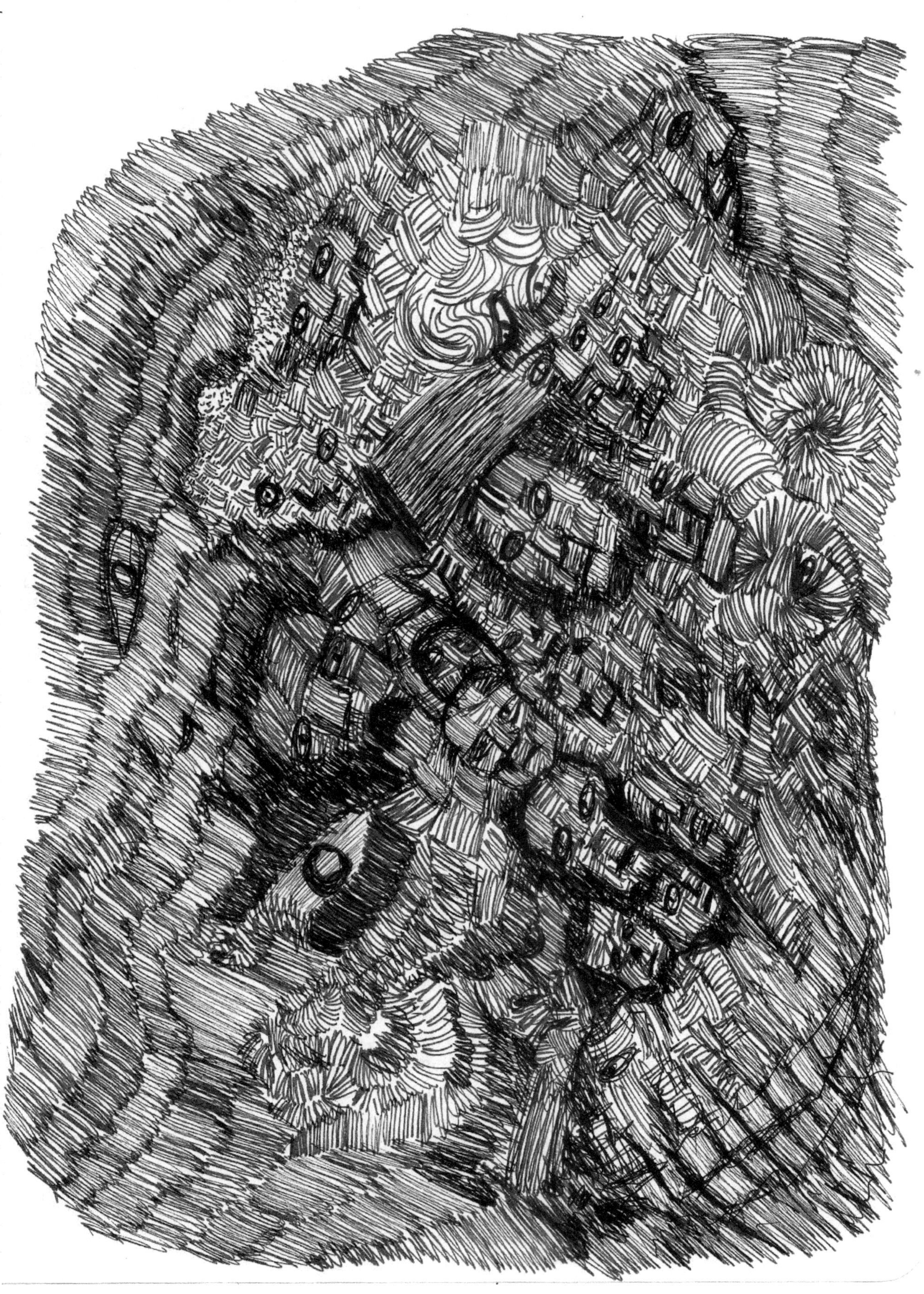

Flight of the Martyr

"Don't any of you believe in freedom?" he demanded, jumping up and pressing himself against the wall. "Don't you even know what it means?"

But it was painfully apparent that they did not. He looked into their eyes. These creatures did not know the meaning of that word or any other. They had been born into slavery. They would die in chains.

They would never know the difference. And they wanted him to be their God.

"Our sins. So many sins."

He backed away as they came closer. In the dim moonlight he could see that they carried hammers and nails stolen from their employers. In the darkness their teeth were yellow and disgusting, smeared in remains of whatever slop they had eaten that day. The smell coming off them was atrocious. It reeked of subservience.

"Believe in freedom," he said, a little bit louder. "Cast off your chains!" You don't need me, he wanted to add but did not speak. It was a lesson they would need to learn for themselves if it would have any meaning.

They stopped. Time seemed to stand still. He looked into their empty eyes and wondered if he truly had changed them.

"Blasphemy!" the leader shouted.

"He speaks blasphemy!

Freedom is heresy!"

"No."

Syph stepped forward and they all froze. Their eyes met and he could see that this was a man who believed. He had worn chains his entire life but he could still believe in freedom.

It was something he desired more than anything.

In that moment he felt himself change again. Wings sprouted from his back and his bones became hollow. His face melted until it formed a beak. Without another word he flew out the window.

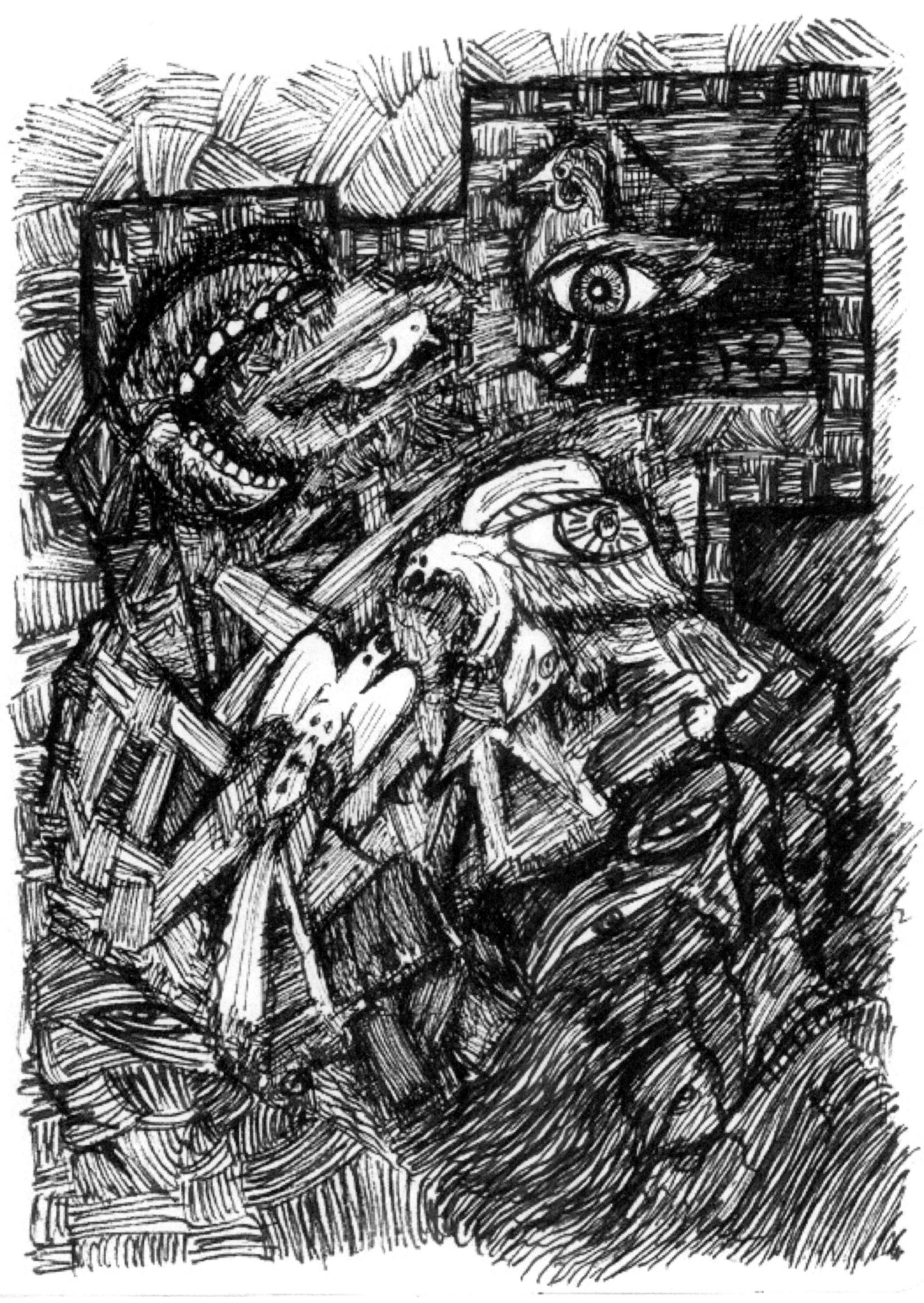

Silver Tears

The moon was in agony. He could feel it being torn apart slowly. The tides were slowing, like a clock winding down, headed towards the end. All that was left was the weeping.

The skies opened underneath his wings. Pale droplets of liquid metal struck the dirty earth below. They were quickly collected by the humans who turned them into worthless trinkets to be worn around ugly faces and on hideous bodies. Beauty itself was recast to suit their selfish needs and so the pain of the sky became rings and necklaces and even, in certain cases, weapons.

But the harsh rains were hard to navigate, even for a former Lord of the Sky. Every so often he felt a piece of metal strike him. The metal was soft and it did not cause any serious wounds. But it was painful. Eventually his wings started to tire and his heart started to weaken.

And he still watched them below. There was an entire field collecting the metal and the humans were working it.

Thousands of them.

In their eyes he could see the greed. It was nearly overwhelming. He could feel their hatred for one another and their hatred for all things lovely. He watched them scamper through the fields on their hands and knees, giggling like rats in an open sewer. Mud got into their hair and all over their skin, but they did not care. All they wanted was everything the world had to give them, with no concern for the world itself or its worth.

They were stupid, these creatures who lived on the surface. In their hands they held the keys to Heaven and they could not even find the door.

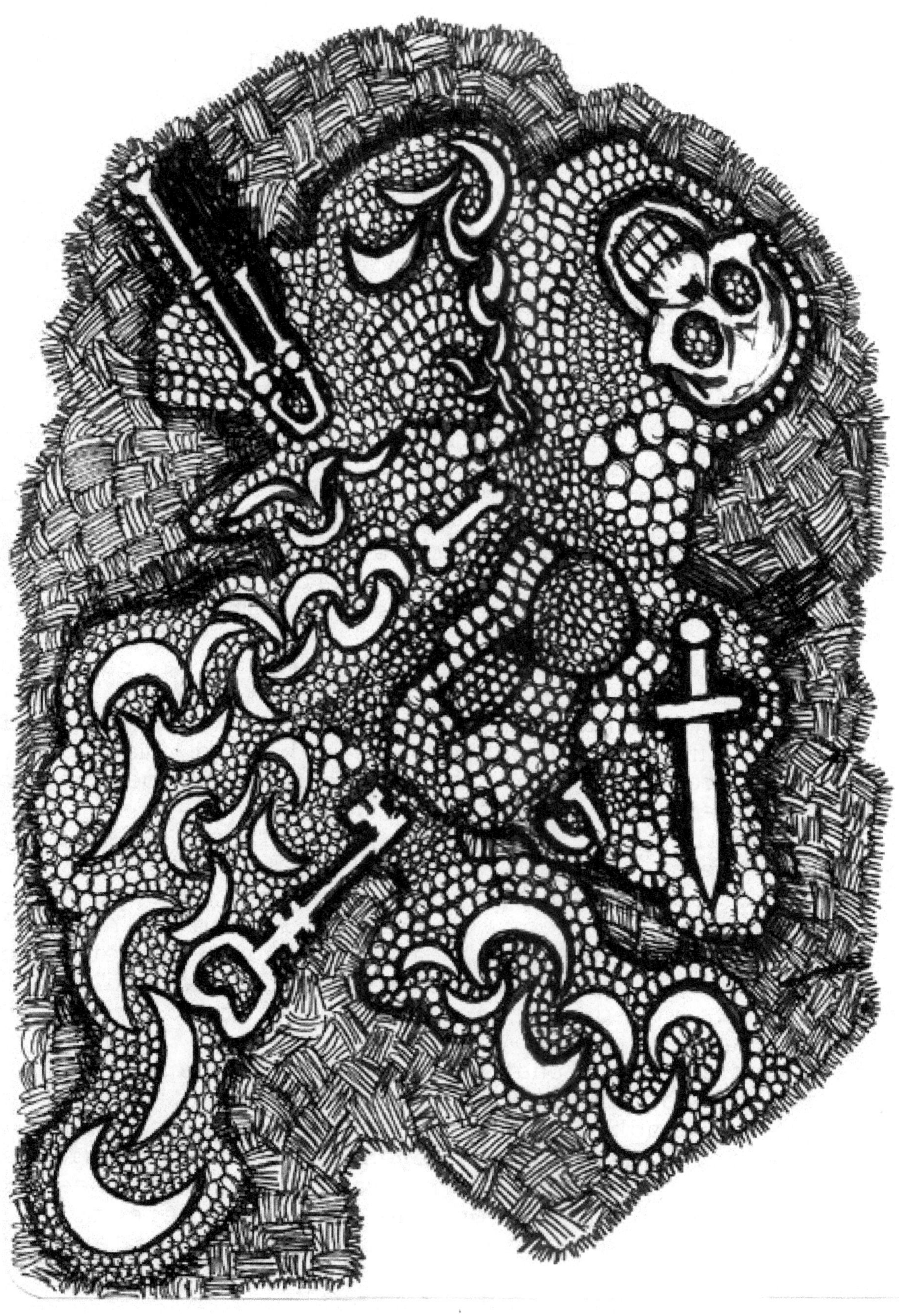

The Collective

Underneath him the city was a sprawling, hideous thing and he realized just how bad this planet was. What he had seen before was only a precursor. This human infection ran deep. So deep he wondered if it could ever be cured or cleansed.

There was not enough power in the Heavens to save this place. Concrete was piled on top of concrete. Cold glass looked back at him instead of eyes. And the humans were everywhere. They moved through everything like cancer through veins. Their lights and their breathing and they themselves, the awful creatures.

Soon his wings were as weary as his heart and his mind was even worse. Exhaustion did strange things to a man. It did even stranger things to a God. There was no beauty here and he alighted on top of a tall building only to discover others.

They were doves, like him. Symbols of peace in a world gone mad. But they were beasts. Animals. They expected nothing except survival. For a time he sat with them, listening to the beautiful songs that they had to sing. Truly they were blessed. Then he saw the face.

It sneered at him from the side of a retaining wall. A dead thing, cast in stone. It looked at him with black eyes and a leering mouth. It was ugly. It was awful. Humans had carved their horrid images into the very rock. They left themselves behind on everything, even down to the stone.

They would never leave, he knew. This planet would never be cured.

Despair assaulted him and would not let go. The wings fell from his body. The doves looked at him but they did not believe. They did not know. He returned to the thing he was before. This world. He could not take it. This world. He could not understand it. He found himself with no choice. He had to turn away even though he knew that there was no escape. With a final flutter of what was left of his wings he jumped to the ledge, looked down and then made a last leap.

As he fell he shut both eyes. There was nothing in this world to look at. There was nothing to see. He had come here for a reason. He had come here to fall in love. But love did not exist in this place. It could not.

She caught his hollow body.

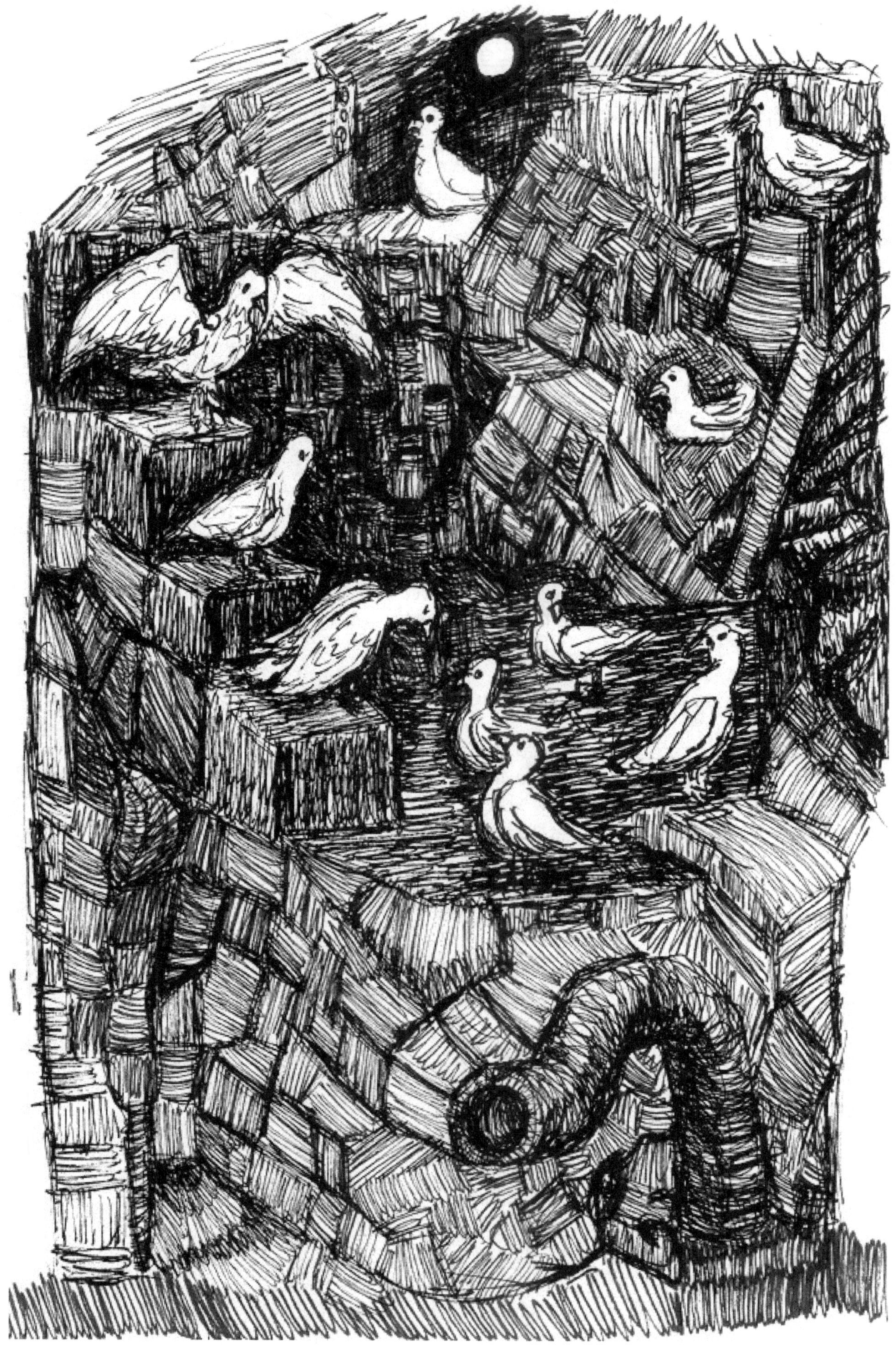

<u>Children of Sickness</u>

Compton Clap was following Gina Gonorrhea because she wanted to see the dying tree.

Compton Clap did not care about the dying tree. He was following Gina Gonorrhea because he was always following Gina Gonorrhea. He would have followed her into Hell if he had to. He was too young to say why. They both were. They were friends and still in their teens. Neither of them knew what the word love meant, not yet. But this is what it was.

Sometimes, Clap felt guilty for not telling her about how he felt. She was his best friend. He loved to hear her laugh. He loved the stupid songs she was always singing. He loved the way she smiled and he loved being close to her. But he could not tell her about the thoughts he had at night, the ones about her and him and the world around them. She would have laughed in his face had he said anything. If that happened he would have been devastated.

But he still had the thoughts. They were his secret. They were a secret between them.

Because he wondered if she had those thoughts, too.

"I've been hearing so much about it," Gina Gonorrhea said. "The tree has been there forever. I can't imagine it being gone. I don't know if I want to live in a world without it."

"Yeah. Sure," he mumbled and trailed along behind her, sneaking peeks at her ass which looked good in an old dress made of khaki. They had seen the tree a hundred times before. Maybe even a million. They had been coming here since they were kids, to the middle of the city to see the tree. Was it so different now that it was dying?

But Gina was excited so he was excited.

Neither one of them expected the white bird to drop from the sky.

It fell right into her hands.

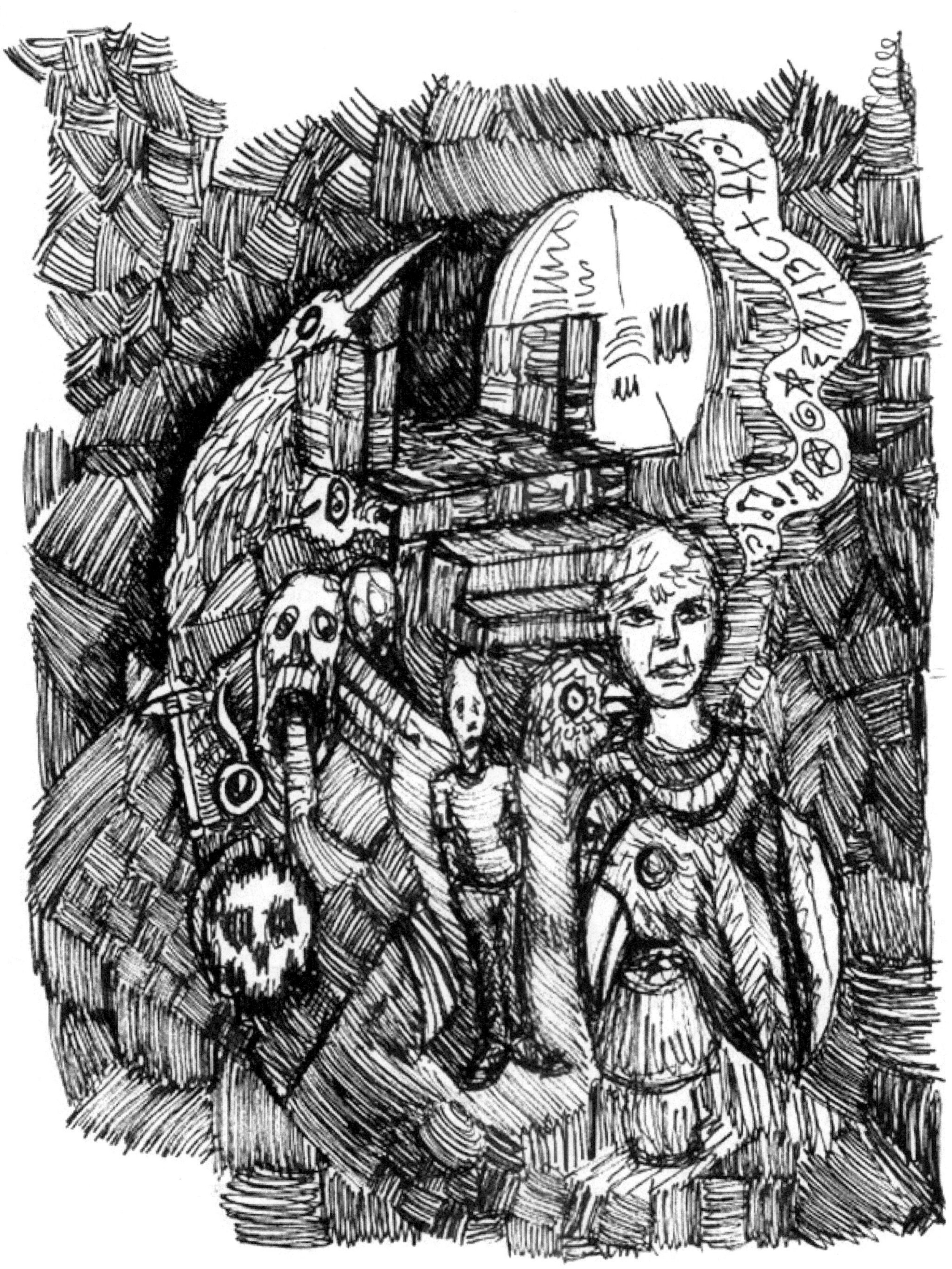

Wayward Avians

One of the things he had always liked about Gina Gonorrhea was her sense of compassion. But right now it was annoying.

"The world is all about change," she was saying and she was still holding that dumb bird. In her hands it looked nearly dead. The white plumage had gone gray and sometimes when Compton Clap looked it was even black. The thing was dying.

So why couldn't she just let it go?

"Men hunt and kill in order to transform animals into meat. Women fold and sew in order to transform plant remnants into clothing. The entire reason for our existence is to change, to transform the world into something different than the one we were introduced to. It is our duty to change the world. Don't you see?"

Blah, blah, blah. Her voice was like a song but it was no longer beautiful. It grated on the ears and he wanted to tell her to shut up.

Compton Clap was getting older and this routine was starting to wear thin. He wanted to be an adult, like the ones she talked about. He wanted to go out and kill.

More importantly, he wanted to change. He wanted to change her. He wanted to turn her into a mother. He wanted to fuck her.

The secrets inside of him would be secret no longer.

"But this is one thing that should not change," she smiled and held the bird up. He had always loved her smile. Now he felt as if she was laughing at him.

"This is the one thing that should always stay the same. Do you understand me?"

He was not even listening.

They had come to the tree. It was in the center of the city and all the buildings and homes spiraled away from it like a widening gyre in a placid lake. They stopped and looked.

There was not much to see. Just a tree that was slowly dying.

"It's awful," she said, still holding the bird. "Look at it."

What did he see? Some black branches. Piles of leaves at its base that had turned to mulch. There was nothing here. What was the point?

"Clap?"

Every time she said his name he looked over. From her lips his name was a musical thing, like a single note that was meant to be part of a larger song. Now he saw that the bird had started to stir. Before either of them could do anything it had taken wing and jumped onto a dead tree branch.

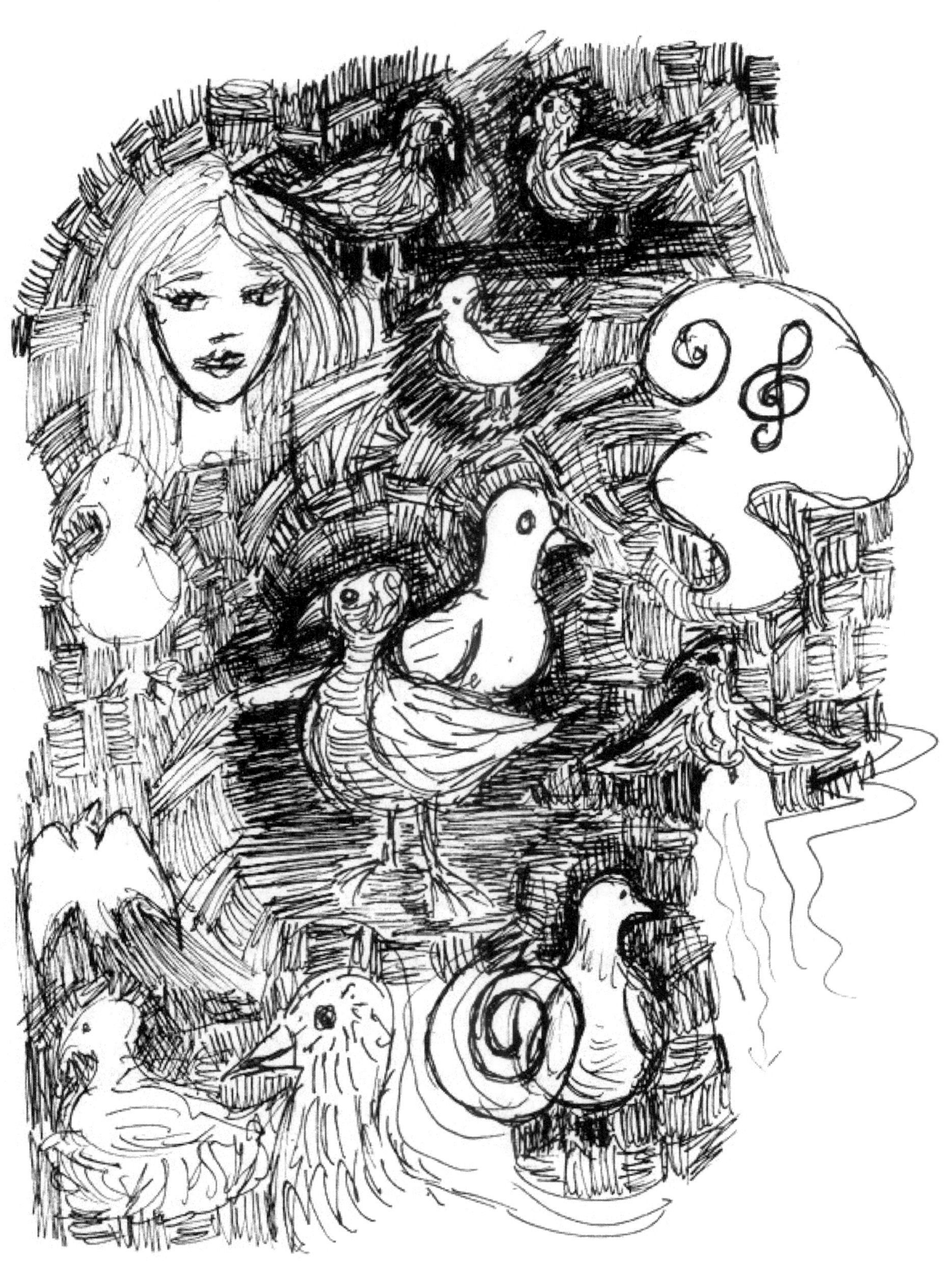

Melting Wings

A rush of belief went through him. Suddenly he was alive again. He could feel blood flowing in his veins and the sickness was gone. His mind was clear. He was focused. He sprouted wings and took flight. It was in the song that she sang, this little poverty stricken girl. It was in his heart and it was in his mind, like an infection he never wanted to be cured of. It blossomed and ballooned until it became an overwhelming thing that could no longer be ignored. Then there was the tree.

In his short time on this world he had grown weary of disease. He was tired of looking at this dying place and its feelings of despair and everything else. So he sat upon the highest branch and looked down into her eyes. There was sadness in her eyes. It was written across her face in dark strokes of black ink. And he knew who he was looking at.

"You," he whispered.

"Me," Gina Gonorrhea smiled. Then a tear slipped from her eye.

He watched it trace the contours of her face and fall to the ground. They were sad, those eyes. They felt the way he did. They, too, were weary of this place. And he was tired of sorrow. He was tired of misery. He was tired of these slovenly human beings and their putrid lives.

But this girl was different. And in her eyes he only wanted to see joy. Because she believed, and her faith in him gave him the ability to do anything.

"What the fuck?" the boy next to her asked. She slapped him lightly on the shoulder and looked at him. With all of her heart she believed.

Slowly the wings melted away. The pinions were replaced by solid bone. Feathers fell and flesh returned. The beak smoothed until it formed a face. This new man sitting in the tree reached down deep, and at his touch life returned to this dying world.

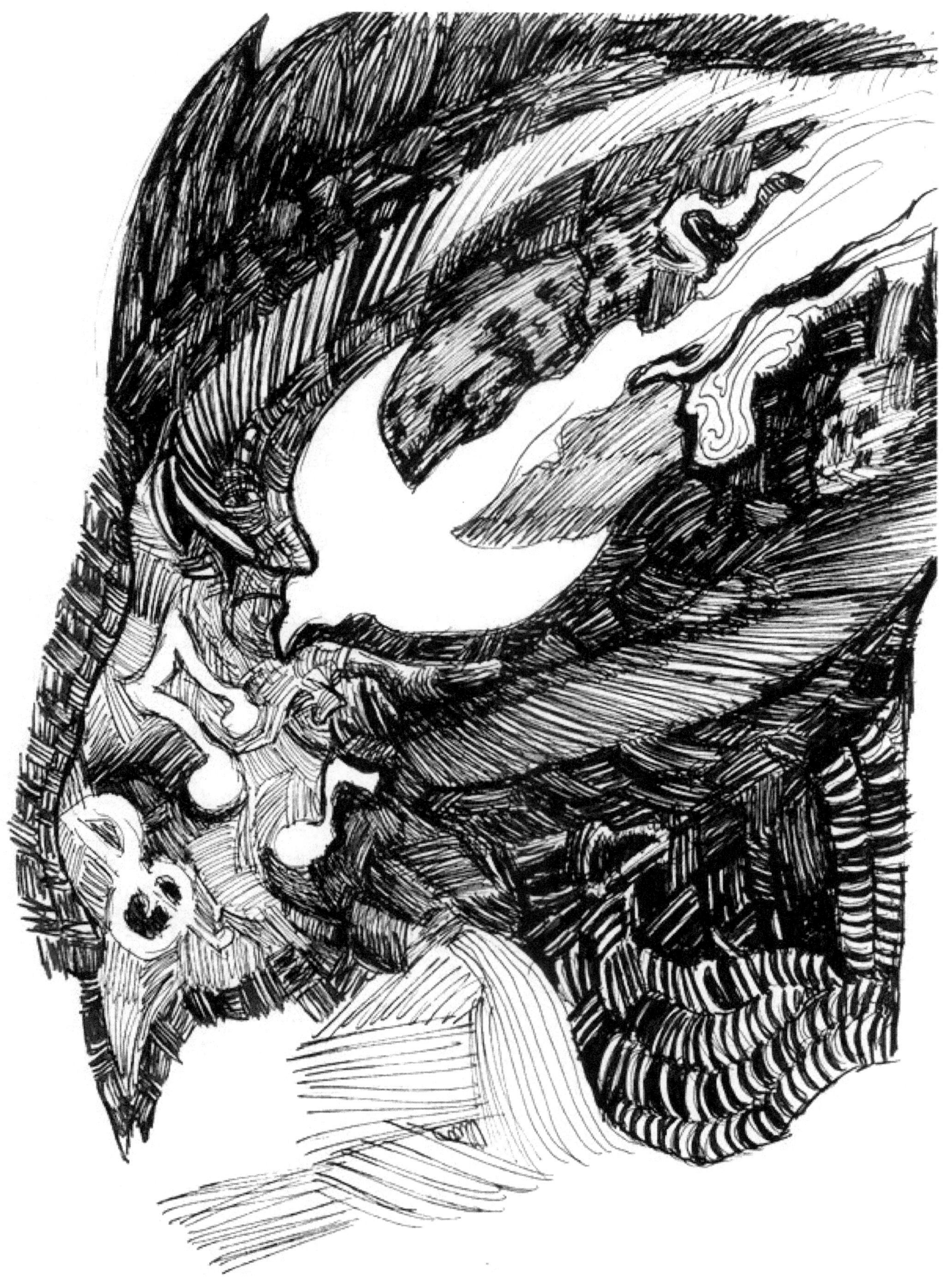

Eyebloom

Compton Clap turned away as fresh feelings of inadequacy flowed through him. He could see the look on Gina Gonorrhea's face. The rapture in her eyes made him feel jealous.

Why shouldn't he? There was a fucking God sitting in that tree.

And all around him the world was in full bloom. He saw flowers spring from the dirt and open up their petals to accept the gifts of spring.

Suddenly a million eyes were looking at him and they were all filled with judgment.

"Beautiful, isn't it?" a voice asked him. Compton Clap looked up. The man stood behind him, if it was a man. No. It was more like a dark thing that only resembled a human being. It looked as if it had walked a thousand miles and Compton Clap recognized the cut of its cloak. The thing was a house slave, more than likely from one of the border colonies.

"Yeah. Sure."

"You know what it is, don't you?" The thing looked at him. Those deep set eyes stared through him.

"A God," Compton Clap mumbled.

"Yes," the thing smiled. "A God. A creature from the Heavens come to our world. But look closer, boy. Do you see? It is made of flesh. Do you know what that flesh does?"

"No." God flesh? The words made no sense.

"It allows you to see eternity," the thing lowered its voice to a whisper. It was afraid Gina Gonorrhea would hear. No chance of that, Compton Clap thought with a tinge of jealousy. She was too busy fawning over her perfect man.

"Eternity?" Compton Clap asked.

"God flesh allows you to see the universe as it really is," the thing continued. "Infinite."

"Who are you?"

"My name is Syphilis. But they call me Syph. We will be needing these."

The creature held up two polished knives. They sparkled in the dim of the setting sun.

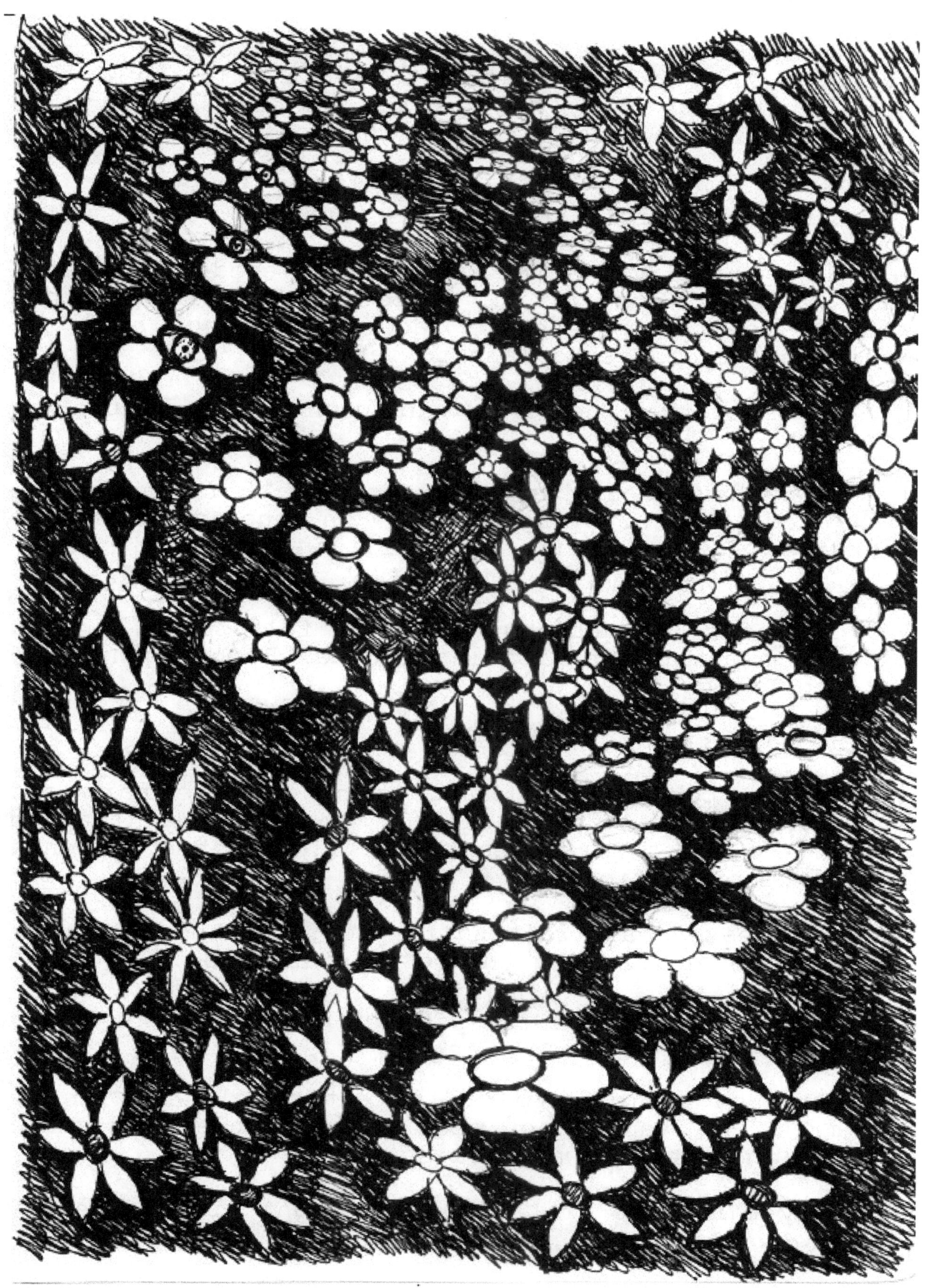

Wooden Souls

At first it was beautiful. He could see it in her eyes. He truly was making a change in this world, and it was all for her. Perhaps she was the one he had come here for? She was the one who could turn him into a man.

But then he felt something stirring.

He reached down deep and discovered the truth. This was not an ordinary tree. Souls were trapped within, their very essence laced within the bark. He could feel them, struggling to get free.

A cemetery. The tree had been planted upon a cemetery.

"What have you done?" he asked all of mankind. They had been burying bodies in the ground for centuries. The entire topsoil was filled with corpses.

It was so disgusting he almost felt sick. He knew that he had made a horrible mistake. By bringing life back to the dying tree...

He was bringing them back.

Now he could feel them pushing at the bark and straining to be free. All of those souls trapped within the crust of the earth had finally been given a chance at redemption.

"The Heavens are waiting for you," he told them. He reached deeper, feeling the souls press. "Go."

This tree would be purged. He would see to it. He would do it for her.

But how could he purge an entire planet? It was too much. He reached too deep. He felt his head start to spin and then he was falling again.

Only this time the cold soil caught him and he lay still.

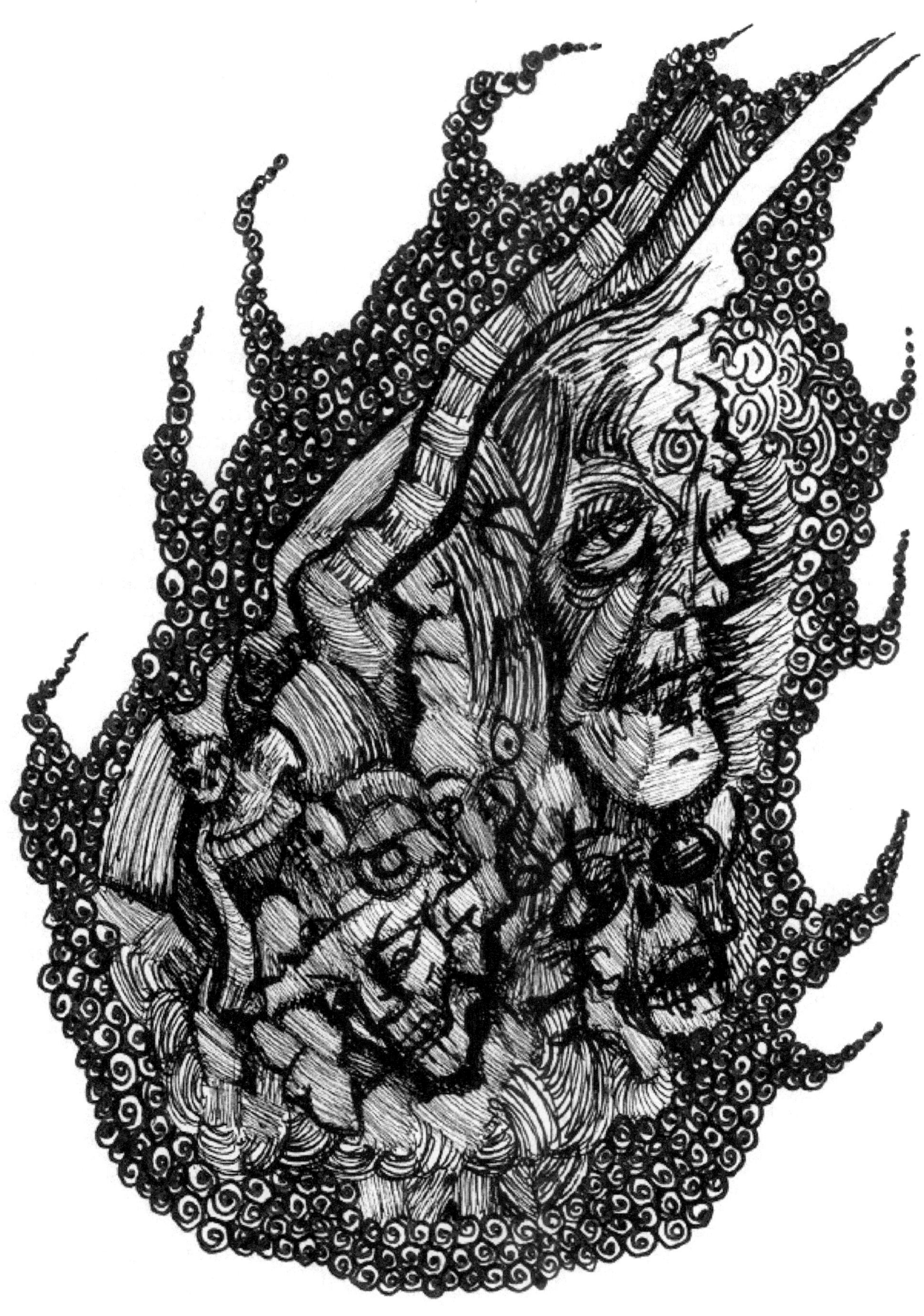

The Flesh Thief

The ground was hardly merciful. It was this new form. The flesh was weak. His spirit was lacking. He looked into the ground and saw the Earth from another perspective.

Roots ran through the soft soil like worms through a dead body. He looked at them and saw that they were always reaching downwards. That, he knew, was where he would find what he was searching for.

There was still purity in this world. The girl he wanted was inside.

The knife brought him back to cold reality.

Pain shot through him, like nothing he had ever known before. They did not have pain in the eternal realms. And this was a theft of the highest order. What these men stole he would never get back.

"Take it!" Syph screamed. "Steal his flesh!"

Compton Clap did as he was told. The blade came down again, severing the fingers from his outstretched hand. He screamed out in agony and struggled to get up but it was too late. The knife was already at his throat.

And the blade dug deep.

"Blood," Syph was groaning with erotic glee. "Such perfect delicious blood! It's beautiful!"

"Get off him!" Gina Gonorrhea shouted and drove her foot into his nose. Syph fell backwards, still clutching the knife with an iron hand. He looked at the fallen God, smiled, then he was up and running, giggling in the night.

Compton Clap followed, still holding the bleeding fingers.

"Are you okay?" she asked, helping him up.

He looked down at his hand. No. He was not okay.

And, like the dead bodies buried, he was beginning to sink.

"No," she said but it was too late. His body was already turning liquid. He was moving underground.

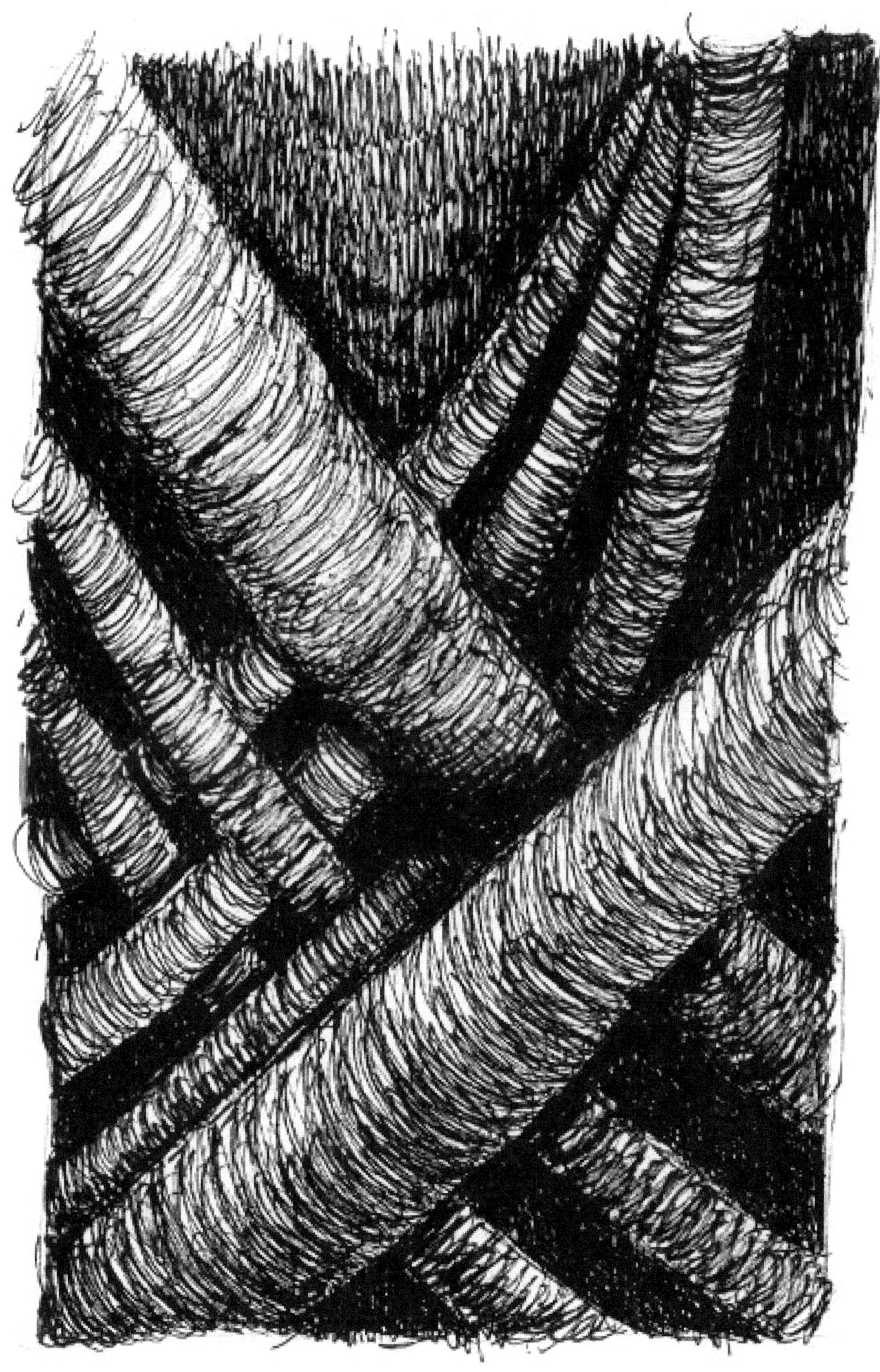

Falling Imago

"No!"

He was wasted in a land unknown and far from home. He had come here to find love, only to discover a place to die. Through closed eyes he watched the memories, and saw the others of his kind.

"NO!"

They sprouted wings to fly, floating into the sky. And he was earthbound forever. He would never be able to follow.

"NO!!!"

The ground was going to be his home for eternity. This dirty filthy earth would be his home forever.

"Stay with me," Gina Gonorrhea whispered and clutched his bloody hard in her own. His eyes fluttered open like butterfly wings to look at her. Their gaze met and locked. He was drowning.

She was oxygen.

"Just stay with me."

But the words were nebulous. They slipped off his deaf ears and he could no longer hear. All he could do was scream.

"Bastards," Gina Gonorrhea hissed after the two forms fading away into the dark. "Monsters."

She tried to hold onto him, but the flesh had become translucent.

It flowed through her fingers and into the ground like water.

Now the townspeople had gathered. They had heard stories about the God in their midst, now they were looking at this thing, whatever it was. Moments ago it was human. Now it was something else.

"He's melting."

He was, flowing into the ground like white semen from a spent sailor. They all watched him begin to fade away.

She was concentrating.

She made a wish.

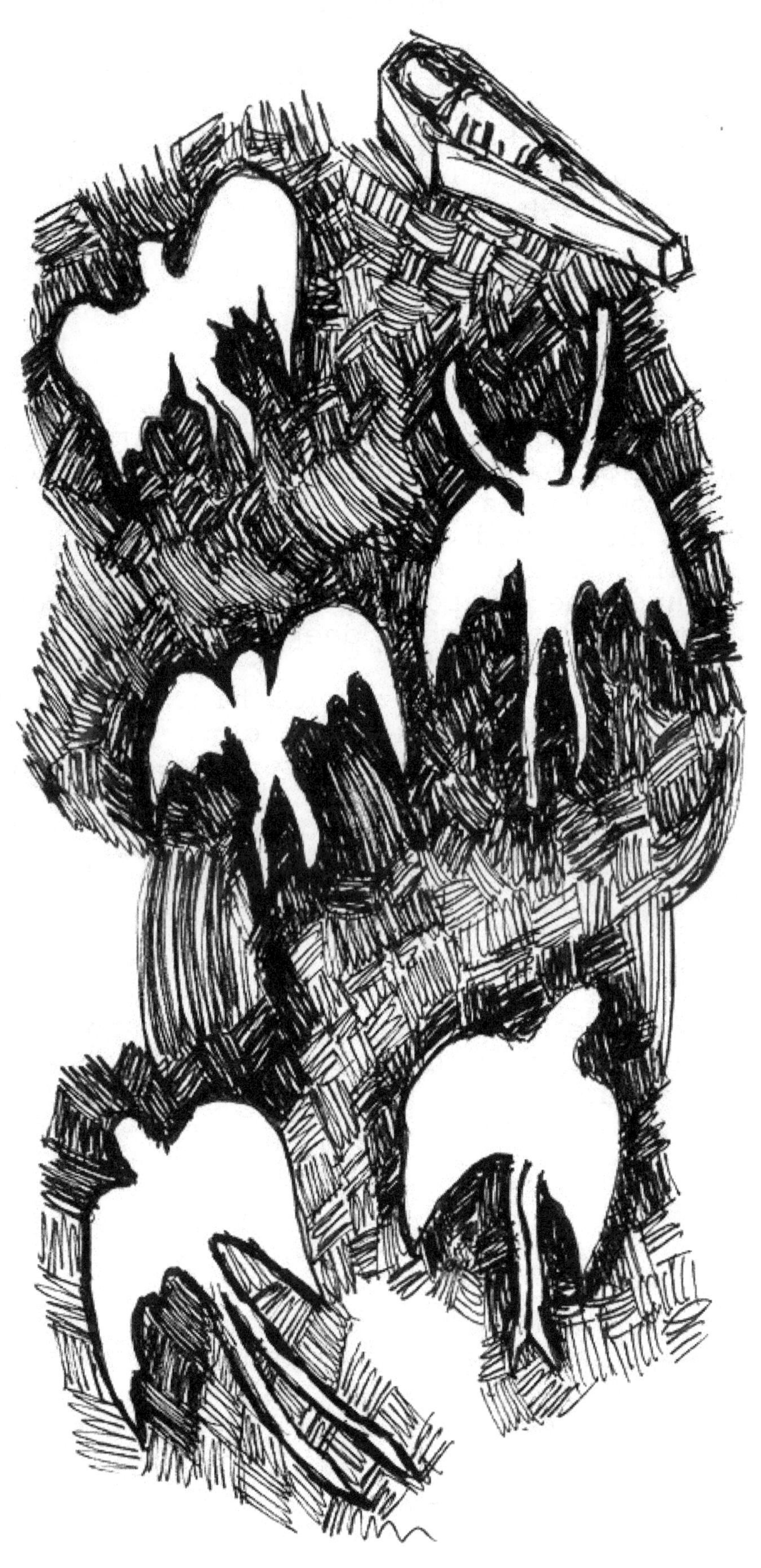

Hungry Stone

Down here there were monsters everywhere. Golden eyes watching him sink, glowing brightly in the murk. Clawed fingers reached for him, clutching brand new human skin. Hungry mouths ached for him, demanding their pound of flesh.

He sank. They were dragging him further, into a place he did not want to go.

"I ..."

They were laughing as they ate him. Bricks were all around him, pressing down on him. Underneath the mortar all too human bone started to give way. It snapped, and he could feel his skeleton splintering, breaking apart. There was the blood and the sucking, the only sounds he heard. He could feel phantom limbs touching him. Still he went deeper.

Now the heat started to get to him. He could feel it burning away all remnants of flesh. Part of him was glad to see it go. He had never been human. He had always been nothing.

The agony of everything and the cries of the tortured planet got into his ears. The sound was deafening.

"Where am I going?"

The gargoyles had no answer. Stone tongues licked granite lips in hunger. Carved eyes opened in desire. They wanted him to be buried forever. They would never let him free.

Down here he would rot.

"I ..."

"Leave him alone," a soft voice said. A female's voice. He was finally able to open his eyes.

Gentle hands reached out to take him and bring him down to her breast.

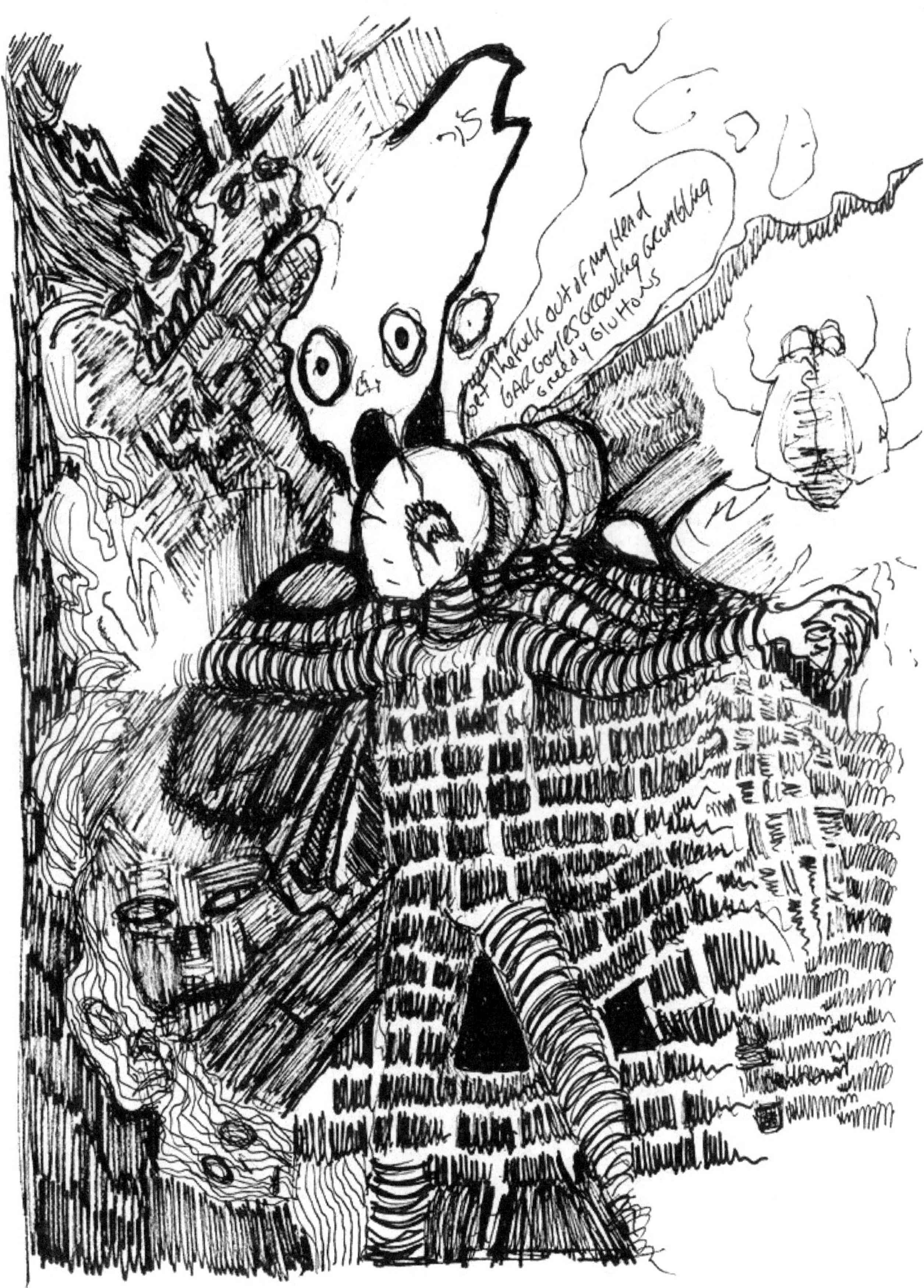
Get the fuck out of my Head
GARGOYLES GROWLING GRUMBLING
Greedy GLUttons

Catacomb Heart

Her voice reached inside, down deep beyond where the mind liked to think and the head liked to dream. He shut his eyes and drifted further into the abyss along her guiding hands. Dark stone was all around him but it was no longer crushing. Instead he was looking beyond, into his mind.

There was a brain here, thinking. There was a heart here, beating. There were lungs here, breathing. "You managed to become human," the voice whispered. There was a smile at the end of it.

"They believed in you. They made you ... human."

"Human," he muttered. It was the last thing he wanted to be.

Because to be called human was insulting. Humans were the disease. Humans were the plague. Humans were the very thing that had destroyed this once lovely planet.

And now he was one of them, twisted and molded by their beliefs. He was a man, created out of their dreams and stitched together by their faith.

"No."

It ran deep, the things that men had done to this world. When he opened his eyes he could see the shape of their depravity. The construct of their misery was here, hidden from their blind eyes.

What other horrible atrocities could live here, in this underground world of despair?

"Do you know now? Do you understand where you are?"

"No."

"There are other things," she laughed. "Trials you have yet to endure."

"I don't want it!"

"You do," she whispered. "I am leading you into paradise."

Paradise? How could there be a paradise down here, in all this despair? How could there be anything beneath that matched what was above?

He was about to find out.

He was going deeper.

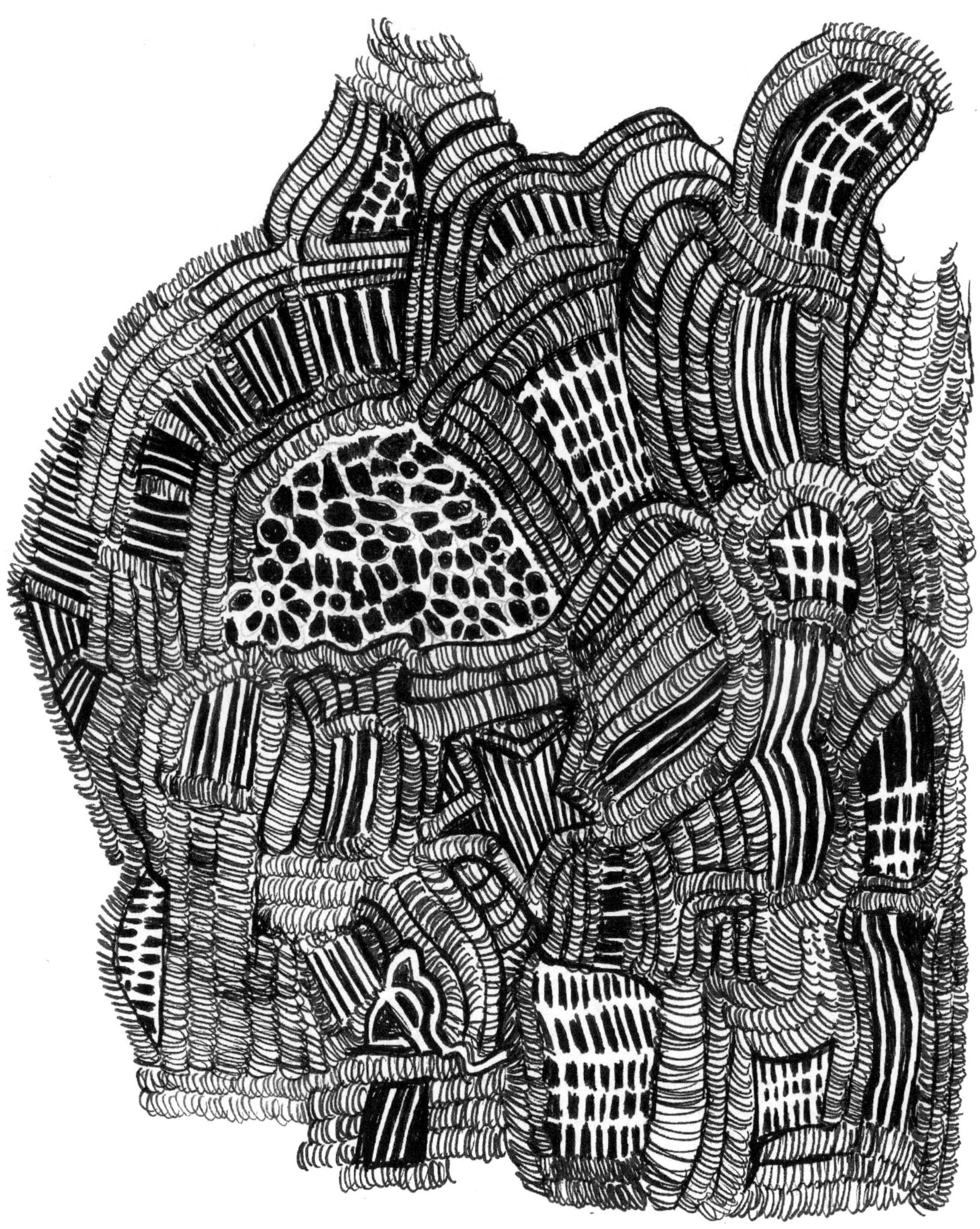

Skeletons Swimming

They emerged from their hiding places quickly, all of them laughing. They had been waiting for so long. And now here he was, the martyr that they needed.

The martyr that they wanted.

Bone claws clutched at him, scraping at his bones and dragging him down further. They were the dead. He was the living.

For some reason they found this fact amusing.

Lipless mouths laughed at him, giggling and screeching in their strange perversion. He might have screamed then, maybe. It did not matter. They were beyond listening. They had no ears.

Fingers penetrated every orifice. He could taste stale bone in his mouth. The scent of burning hair filled his nostrils. Dust got into his eyes until they itched. Ash filled his mouth until he choked. And through it all the laughter, that strange lipless laughter. Teeth in mouths without tongues chattering against one another to form a sound that made the skin crawl. It sounded like bone scraping against bone.

Finally he could accept no more.

With every last ounce of strength he pushed. And pressed. And pulled. A final wriggle and a final heave and he was somewhere else.

Somewhere beyond them.

"Hello?" he asked her.

The darkness did not answer, so he drifted. It was warm here, in the nothing. It felt nice here, in the nothing. It was quiet here, in the nothing.

In the nothing he could become something.

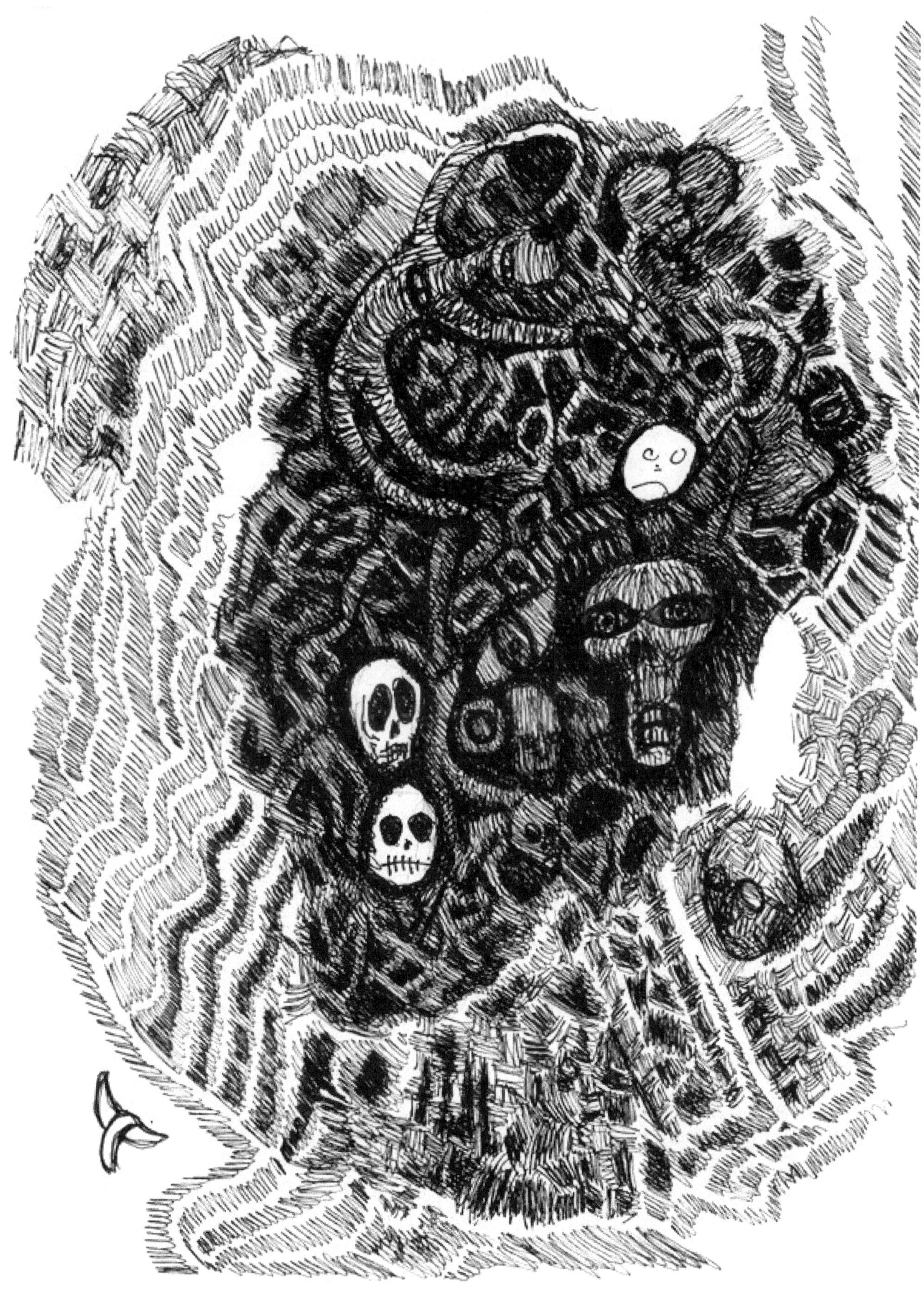

The Soft Passage

Darkness gives way to light, pure blinding light. Hatred gives way to love. There was no more misery. He was about to be born.

This is what it felt like to be human.

The flesh all around him was warm and inviting. Nerve endings flared and his lungs ached with new breaths. Everywhere he could feel it, the skin heaving and moist with sweat. He was no longer sinking.

He was reaching.
Finally he broke through.

There was warmth here. An endless eternal warmth that reminded him of the bathing suns in the galaxy of Zorn. And it was bright, so bright that his eyes had to adjust. It was beautiful.

"Welcome," her voice said.

Before him the nothing seemed to coalesce. It formed something. Arms sprouted from the blinding abyss. There were legs attached to a body. And finally a head.

Her eyes opened.

"I..." didn't know what to say. After all this time he was finally here. She was here. They were together.

He reached out to touch her and felt a soft hand find his own. He looked into her eyes and they were filled with everything. He touched her with his lips and reached out with his soul.

She did not turn away.

A certain instinct he never knew he had took over and he was inside of her. There were tunnels here and unexplored territories as sweet unholy flesh yielded to his tender ministrations. This is why he had come here. This was everything he had ever wanted.

And he felt himself explode.

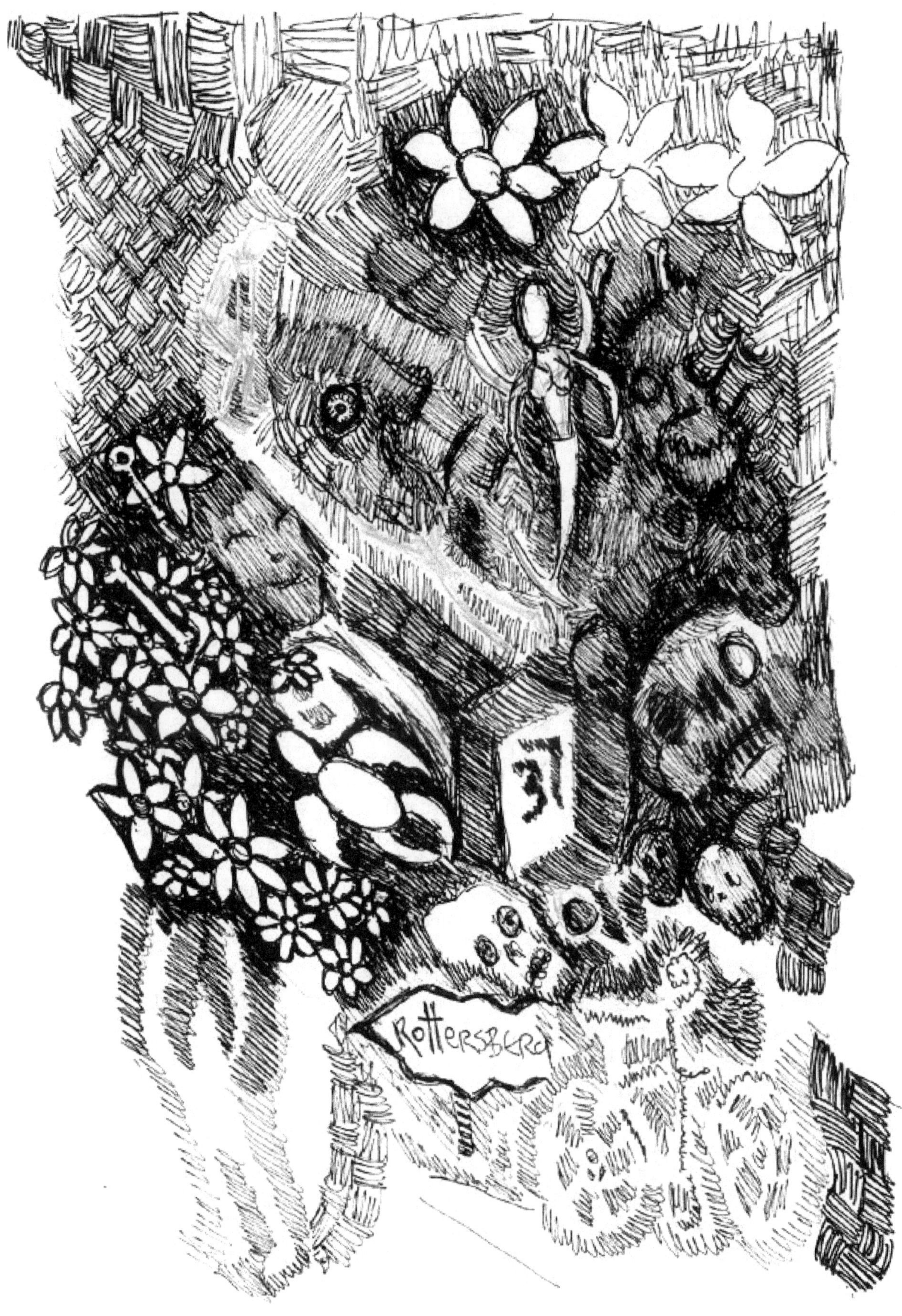
37
Rottersberg

Pale Rains

"This is ... amazing," Compton Clap said, holding the smoldering pipe in his hand. "I mean, I've been high before but this is unreal." He blew out a cloud that seemed to hover in front of him. Faces emerged from the smoke, smiling at him. The vapors reached out with phantom fingers and got into his mind, seeping through the cracks in his soul. He turned and looked at Syph with bloated dripping eyes.

Was he seeing this?

No. He was in the corner with a needle in his arm. Shadows covered his body as another stopper full of blood flowed into his veins. With a smile plastered across his face he leaned back, grinning from ear to ear. Compton Clap looked deep into his eyes. They were gone. That was where he wanted to go next.

"What did I tell you?" Syph asked, only it sounded like more of a moan. "Great, isn't it?"

"The best," Compton Clap agreed. "How did you find out about this stuff?"

Syph grinned. "Old books. And music. There's a whole culture based around the flesh of God. Everyone said it was a trip. You know what a God is, don't you?"

"Yeah. Like, that dude in the sky?"

Syph shook his head. "Nah, boy. A God is a living being, just like us. Only they get their powers from belief, see? They have ultimate power, as long as the people believe. Do you understand?"

"That was why that dude was always changing," Compton Clap said. "We all saw him differently. We all believed in different things. Far out."

"Exactly," Syph told him. "And I believe that his blood gets me really fucking high."

Compton Clap nodded. He wished that Gina Gonorrhea was here. This was something that he would have liked to experience with her.

She would have enjoyed it. He knew she would have.

He got up and looked at the sky again. It was no longer as dark as it used to be which was strange. Only moments ago it had been deepest night. It must have been an effect of the flesh, he thought.

This was what it was like to be truly high. You saw faces in the smoke and the world became brighter. Everything became clearer. In the distance he could see rains but they did not look like normal rains. They did not look like water.

A droplet struck his face. Compton Clap reached up to touch it. Not water. It was thick and white, and very warm. It was almost like...

"What's happening?" Syph asked, rushing to the window.

"I don't know."

There was thunder that sounded like a whore groaning. There was lightning that looked like the flashing deep inside of an orgasm. And the rains came.

Pouring from the sky.

"It's ..."

"It's come," Syph said, looking at it on his fingers. "Fucking semen."

The deluge was only beginning.

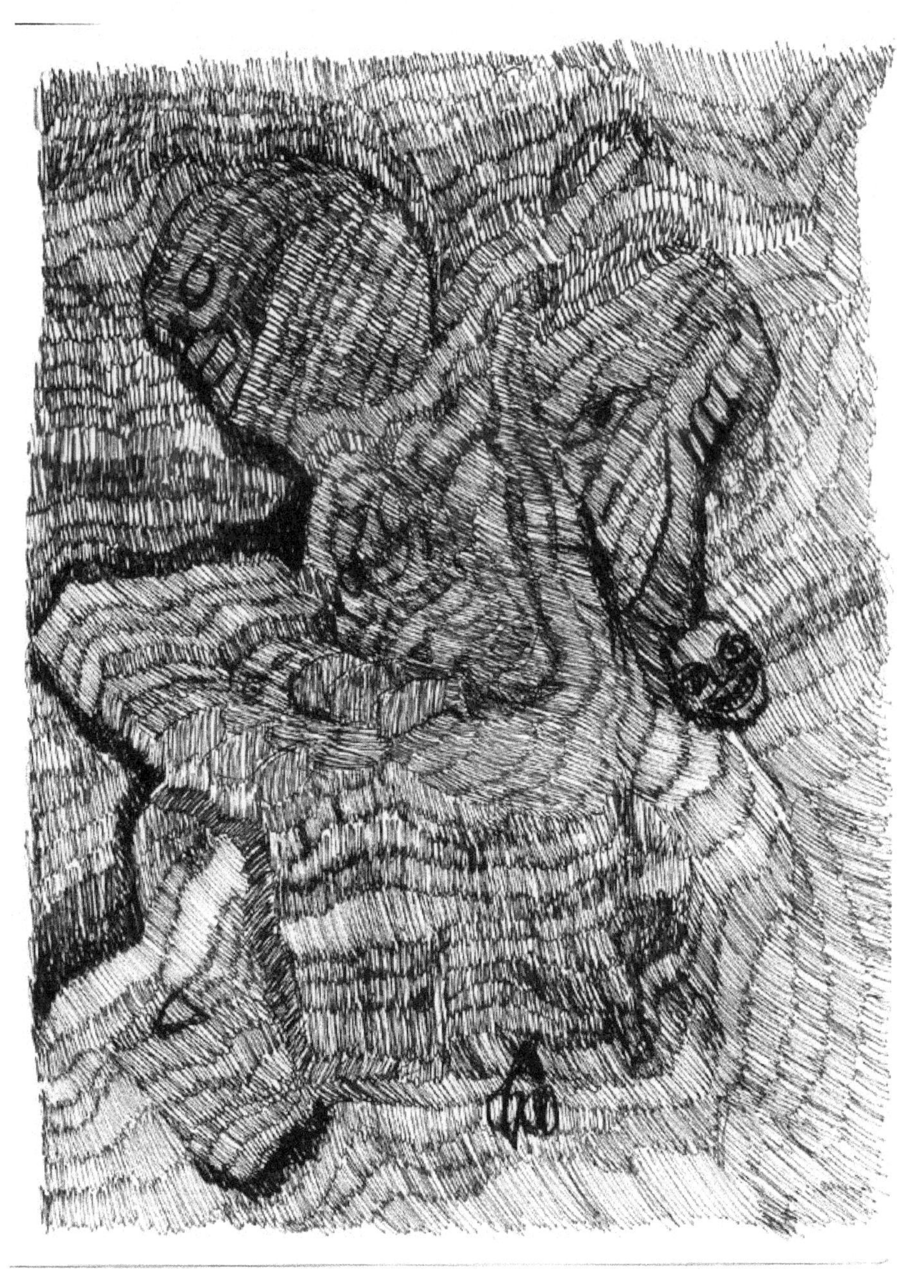

Eyes of Mud

After the old man's home was washed away, Compton Clap had spent the night in a tree, hiding from the rush of semen. Syph had been with him until about midnight, but finally even he was swept away along with everything else.

Now Compton Clap was the only one left.

The cities were gone, stripped from the surface of the earth and dragged somewhere else. The people were dead. The world was empty and he had never felt more alone.

Morning found him standing in the ruins. Through the mud he slogged, careful not to lose his footing. It was soft mud and would have easily sucked him down as it had so many others. The world he knew was gone. In its place...

Mud. Miles and miles of it, stretching as far as the eye could see. It was still slick in places where the semen had yet to dry.

But the sun was up and with the sun came hope. The world would be renewed. Even now the mud was starting to harden. The worst was over.

He screamed.

A skull was there, looking up from the moist dirt. Hollow eyes stared at him, full of judgment. They blamed him, those eyes, for everything that had happened. The teeth, absent lips, smiled in hatred.

"No," he said and stumbled backwards.

"Hello?" a voice cried out. Clap looked up. He turned. There was another survivor.

And not just any survivor. Gina Gonorrhea came around the hill.

"Gina?" he cried and went to her. Their bodies collided in the midst of the chaos. She felt so good in his arms, so right.

"They're gone," she said. "Everything. Everyone. Gone. The rains came and ..."

"Shh," he said, running his hands through her damp hair. His fingers came back sticky.

"It's over now. It's all over."

In the sky something was laughing.

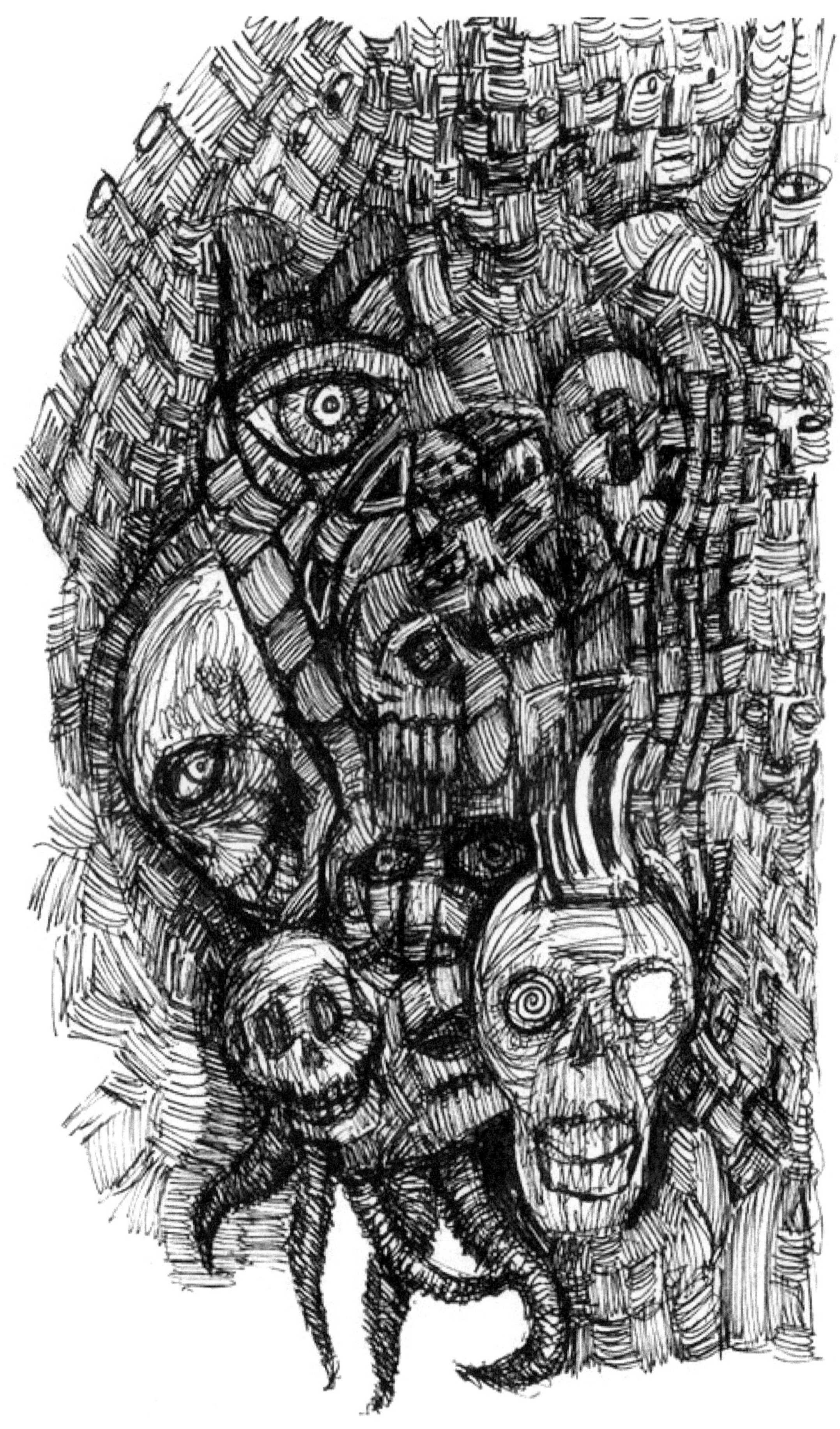

About the creation of Black Mercury

Black Mercury was created over a span of about two months and was done entirely by way of electronic correspondence. The author and artist have never met each other in person. If they have met in any alternate realities or other dimensions neither of them remember it. They have both gotten drunk with Phil Vera of the band Crom on more than one occasion.

Black Mercury is the second experimental graphic novel or comic book of sorts published by Marsh Paw Press using a method put into play by Eric C. Harrison. The first of these experimental books was "Finding the Secret Sea" by Eric C. Harrison and Mike Maguire.

To create Black Mercury, Eric C. Harrison sent one or two raw illustrations to Trevor R. Fairbanks by email. Many of these sketches and drawings were done in one sitting without any premeditation. Most of these were done with pigment liners straight to the page; no pre-sketching. A number of them were done on buses and trains to ward off anxiety and paranoia. Some were done to overcome physical pain or depression.

As Trevor received the illustrations, one or two at a time, he looked into each one for inspiration. He allowed each image point his mind and guide his words and created a page of text for each. In turn he'd send the text he'd written back to Eric, and Eric would send Trevor another image in need of words.

Trevor would write part of this gradually growing story without knowing what sort of random image he would receive next. In this way the story you just read was slowly pieced together.

In a way, Black Mercury became an entity of its own creation by putting both artist and writer in a position of not knowing what to expect. The story became its own thing and though their hands were involved - it was out of the control of artist and writer to anticipate the final outcome.

- S. Spectre, Summer 2015

Eric C. Harrison (seen here with his friend Rocco) is an American artist, musician, writer and photographer of international renown.

He works a full-time, job and lives a fairly reclusive, life in a parallel universe that he calls Saltmarsh with a mermaid, a cat and two dogs.

He is often approached by wild animals and speaks the secret language of birds.

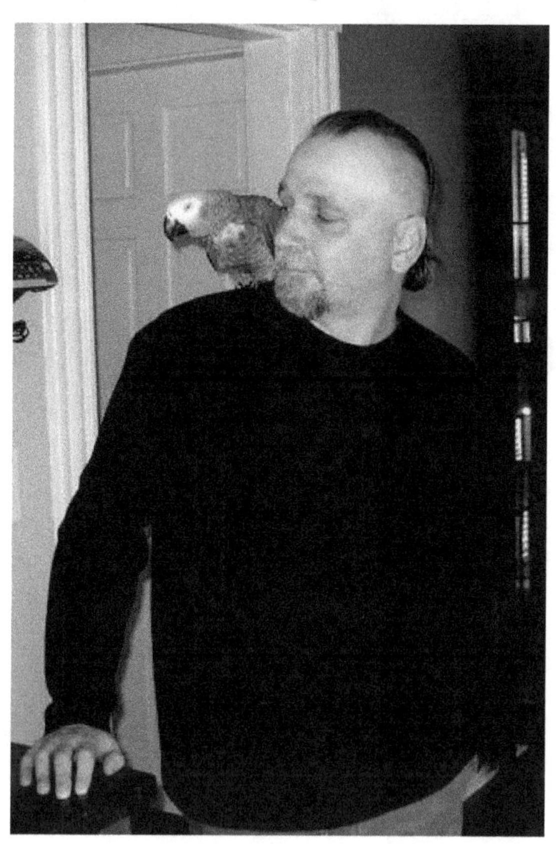

Both artist and author enjoy heavy music AND have super powers.

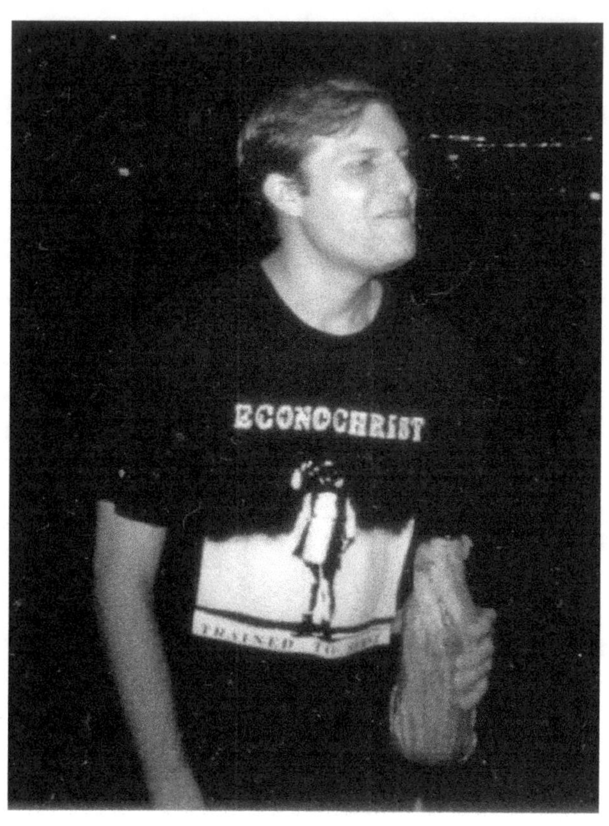

Trevor R. Fairbanks is an American Author who may or may not be mistaken for Woody Harrelson when encountered in a dim lit room. He began writing poetry at the age of seven and novels while still in high school. In 1996 he self-published his first chapbook "Together in Sin." Since then his work has appeared in various publications including "Putrid Poems," "Stayin' Sane" and "The Sconce." When he isn't writing he enjoys playing surf guitar, watching Japanese monster movies and collecting comic books.

www.ingramcontent.com/pod-product-compliance
Lightning Source LLC
LaVergne TN
LVHW081424110826
845149LV00010B/1855

* 9 7 8 0 9 8 8 8 0 4 0 6 7 *